Insanity Plea:

A Teenager's Journey Navigating the Judicial and Mental Health Systems with a Mental Health Disorder,

Told through His Mother's Eyes

"It is more important to know the patient who has the disease than the disease the patient has." - Hippocrates

LaShawne Houston Sowell, LMSW
& Frederick D. Sowell Jr.

LaShawne Houston Sowell

Copyright © 2019 by Lashawne Houston Sowell LMSW

All rights reserved. This book or any portion thereof may not be reproduced or used in any manner whatsoever without the express written permission of the publisher except for the use of brief quotations in a book review.

Printed in the United States of America

First Printing, 2019

ISBN: 9781097458998
Imprint: Independently published

Acknowledgments

"I can do all things through Jesus Christ who gives me strength."

- Philippians 4:13

The most supportive brother in the universe, Donald Houston, who would often drive from Philadelphia to Connecticut to assist whenever and wherever he could.

The rest of my immediate family, my automatic internal inspirations - Daughter, LaKeisha, son, Frederick-co-author of this book, Donald's wife, Brecia, Big Fred, Cousin Leroy Clemons, and Mom, Eileen Houston.

My "Writing Buddies" Bunita Keyes and Lauren Gibson, with whom I met with at least monthly to share, write, and edit stories. Your support was more appreciated than you probably know as we discussed very sensitive issues.

Editor- Vangella Buchanan of The Writery Ink, LLC, for her motivation, "Know How To Get it Done" spirit, and technical support.

James, of Humble Nation, for the design cover.

LaShawne Houston Sowell

TABLE OF CONTENTS

Acknowledgments — iii

Prologue — 1

Chapter 1
A Mind in Psychosis — 2

Chapter 2
Raising Awareness — 6

Chapter 3
The Day as I Saw It — 10

Chapter 4
The Phone Call — 12

Chapter 5
The Hartford Court — 14

Chapter 6
The Prison — 15

Chapter 7
The Judicial System, and Attorney # 1 — 18

Chapter 8
More Court — 21

Chapter 9
The Release — 23

Chapter 10
Institute of Living — 28

Chapter 11
The First Discharge — 29

Chapter 12
The Probation Officer — 31

Chapter 13
Uncle John — 33

Chapter 14
> The End of Attorney # 1   35

Chapter 15
> Attorney # 2   37

Chapter 16
> Court Continues   39

Chapter 17
> Dad's Sudden Death   42

Chapter 18
> The Slave Bracelet Again   45

Chapter 19
> Diversion Program Denied   46

Chapter 20
> The Media   49

Chapter 21
> Now What?   51

Chapter 22
> The Public Service Officials   54

Chapter 23
> Back to Court Again   56

Chapter 24
> The Mental Health Defense   58

Chapter 25
> The Trial   60

Chapter 26
> The Forensic Institute   62

Chapter 27
> Back to Court Again   66

Chapter 28
> The Judge Had No Clue (The Verdict in

Review) 67

Chapter 29
    The First Episode 69

Chapter 30
    Back to the Forensic Institute 74

Chapter 31
    "The Jail for White Privilege? " 76

Chapter 32
    Money, Power, Greed 78

Chapter 33
    The Psychiatric Review Board 79

Chapter 34
    NAMI 84

Chapter 35
    Dante Remains in The Forensic Institute 86

Chapter 36
    The Burden of The Forensic Institute 89

Chapter 37
    Stress Relief Date 91

Chapter 38
    The Legal Rights Project 92

Chapter 39
    A Less Restrictive Setting 93

Chapter 40
    Advocacy Unlimited 95

Chapter 41
    The Senator 97

Chapter 42
    Corruption and the Abuse Investigation 99

Chapter 43
> The Karuna Conference   100

Chapter 44
> The Emotional Distress   101

Chapter 45
Race and Racism   103

Chapter 46
The Insanity Plea: Afterthoughts   106

Chapter 47
Planning For Dante To Come Home   108

Chapter 48
Broken Hospitals & Mental Health Systems   109

Chapter 49
Dante's Day Ones   110

Epilogue
The Fight Continues   111

About the Authors   113

Prologue

The following story was not physically difficult for me to write; however, it was emotionally difficult as the issues of race and mental illness can be uncomfortable ones to discuss, especially when it affects your own family. It has been cathartic for me to write this story as fiction based on very real events. I have been able to put the combined issues of race, justice, and mental health into some perspective. The combination of these issues does affect many in our society.

I started writing this story, and about a year into writing, editing and rewriting, the issues of mental health and corrupted systems became forefront surface issues in our country and in the media. I have addressed these very real problems in the final chapters of this book but felt the need to share the following story first.

The following is the story of a young man, Dante, whose struggles with mental illness went unnoticed, until one day, he had a major episode. His parents woke up to this reality as they found themselves struggling to understand all that was happening and how they had arrived at this point. Dante's story is one that is repeated all across the nation, and for young black males, it resonates like a loud echo.

Getting into the mind of an individual with mental health issues can be a scary journey. What is even more scary is the system's response to the individual and its treatment of the individual and families. I know because I am Dante's mother, but I will begin with his story, because it really is *his* story.

Chapter 1
A Mind in Psychosis

In late September 2014, as he has now written a hip-hop song about, Dante had a psychotic episode that would change his life forever.

In Dante's own words:

> On September 28th, I committed a "crime."[1] I was suffering from a combination of both psychotic and manic symptoms. During this time, I was having paranoid delusions. I felt as if I was being watched and tested by the federal government or people who are considered "higher ups" who deal with government operations. I felt people in my community were being paid off by these government officials to poke fun at me because I believed that I had prophetic and occult powers at the time.
>
> My delusional thinking led me to believe that one day, in the near future, I was going to use these powers to take down the evil higher ups and powerful corrupt establishments of the world. My mental health began to further deteriorate when I started to have delusions that I was receiving personal messages from the television and radio. These messages affirmed the false powers.
>
> I was working a third shift job at the time and the work was extremely demanding. At work, I thought that the company

---

[1] A crime-the act of doing something criminal must, with certain exceptions, be accompanied by the intention to do something criminal. Wikipedia

was symbolic of the evil establishment. I quit the job after just a few weeks of working due to its great demands and the paranoia that I was feeling.

The next day, the crime occurred; it was a Sunday. I was already delusional. I attended church with my mother. There were a lot less people in attendance. I thought that the normal church-goers stayed home, because somehow, they knew that I would be there, and they were scared that there might be a plot against the church by the government due to my presence. To clarify, they were not after the church goers; they were all after me.

I thought once the pastor began to speak, his sermon was subliminally directed towards me. I did think that the pastor knew of my prophetic powers and was trying to warn or protect me from the "higher ups" and what they were going to do to me. While in church, I asked my mother if I could put on the shades that I brought to church. At the time, I thought the shades symbolized that I was enlightened when I wore them and that the pastor would receive the message that I knew he was subliminally speaking to me.

My mother rejected my request to wear the shades. I told her that I needed to leave and that I would wait for her in the car until the end of the service. I believed leaving the church would give the pastor a signal that I was not scared and was prepared to fight against the evil "higher ups." I played a Michael Jackson CD while I waited for my mom to come out of church. I felt that Michael Jackson had the same problem with the establishment that I was now having. Of course, he had prophetic powers as did many other celebrities that died too soon. All of their establishments were threatened before they died.

My psychosis and delusional thinking led me to believe that I was constantly being watched by audio and video surveillance. Playing the Michael Jackson CD at the time was a way of showing the "higher ups "that I was on to them. My mother returned to the car and we drove home listening to Michael Jackson. I was somewhat surprised that she did not change the CD to gospel, as this is what she would usually do on Sundays.

On the way home, I asked my mom if we could stop by the corner CVS Pharmacy so that I could purchase some Oreos. I went into CVS, and just like the church, it was extremely empty. The few people that were in the store seemed to be in disguise. They seemed like they were on my side though. They were going to assist me in taking on the "higher ups".

I went to the cookie aisle and noticed the Oreos were on sale, buy one get one free. I thought that this was all part of the plan. The "higher ups" we're trying to make me physically weaker and out of shape. As I exited the store, I threw one of the boxes away to symbolize that I was on to the "higher ups" and I am getting tired of their mind games.

After returning home, I asked my mother if I could go back to the store because I forgot something. She did not want to transport me, so I walked. I walked up the hill about 3 blocks away. I was definitely psychotic and delusional by this time. I felt that all of the people that I passed by on my walk were staring at me and they were jealous because they knew that I had special powers and that I had been divinely chosen to lead the revolution.

I reached the store, and the sports drink that I was looking for was out of stock. I thought that this was also part of the "higher ups" plan. They were continuing to play these mind games. I purchased ginger ale instead. I even felt that this was symbolic.

A family friend was killed earlier that year due to gun violence and his name was Jerale. Instantly, the two names sounded alike. I purchased the soda and poured it out immediately after leaving the store. This was to symbolize the loss of Jerale's life and to let the "higher ups" know that I knew what they were thinking about doing to me, but I was not afraid.

In my continued manic and psychotic state, I did not feel like returning home, so I continued to walk. I walked until I reached the graveyard in the next town over. I now understand that entering the graveyard was yet another symbol. It further emphasized and symbolized not being afraid of death.

In the graveyard, I listened to music from my iPhone 6 that I had recently purchased. The music had subliminal messages that connected me to the revolution that was about to occur. The songs seemed to be speaking directly to me. I began to dance with joy in the graveyard. The message in the music seemed to give me more confidence of the notion that my powers were real.

I began to become angrier and more frustrated because I was having a mix of delusional feelings and psychosis. I began to walk very fast. I kept my shades on as a symbol to the people that I passed by. The shades were supposed to indicate that I was mad that the people were not being honest with me. They knew that I was a prophet; why weren't they treating me as such?

A car pulled up in front of me and stopped. My continued delusions led me to believe that the car was undercover and sent by the "higher ups" to scare me. I believed the "higher ups" were watching me in the graveyard. The "higher ups" were scared themselves because I was receiving messages through the music that they did not want me to know about.

An older woman got out of the car to tend to a gravesite. She left the door open, and the keys were in the car. The car was also left running. I believed the woman was also undercover and she was a symbol that the "higher ups" were on their way to kill me. At this point, I had to prove that I was not afraid. I was definitely tired of the mind games. I rushed into the driver's seat of the car while the lady's back was turned. To my surprise, another person was in the passenger's seat. She immediately exited the vehicle out of fear.

I quickly accelerated. The older woman at the gravesite was now alerted of the situation and rushed back to the car. She attempted to pull me out of the car, but it was too late. I began to drive the car at high speed. In my psychotic state, I felt that I was on a joy ride.

Suddenly, while I was driving, a group of people appeared right in front of me. I was shocked. I did not expect them. I slammed on the brakes to avoid any collisions with the group. I have since been told that this group was a family of mourners. A few men rushed over to the car that I had taken. They were very angry.

Even in my psychotic state, I did not intend to hurt anyone, so I then became afraid. I knew that I had found myself in a dangerous predicament. I tried to reverse the vehicle to get away from the angry men. I began to drive away from them. The men quickly got in their cars and proceeded to follow me. I stopped the vehicle in the graveyard, got out, and started running.

The men got out of their vehicles and chased me on foot. The men caught me after I fell to the ground. Upset and angry, they attacked me. While on the ground, I tried to apologize for what had just happened. I heard the older lady shout at the men to stop hitting me. The cops then arrived, and the men stopped their assault. I heard one man shout, "that's him!" The cops took me into custody. I was later notified that a little girl was hit but sustained only minor injuries. My mom said that she was told that no one was hurt. The police report actually said that the little girl was not hurt at all, which the family did later confirm.

Chapter 2
Raising Awareness

After deciding to begin with Dante's own story in his own words, I felt that it would be important to further explain mental health disorders/conditions and how one's brain chemistry could become imbalanced.

Before Dante's last psychotic episode, I had surface knowledge of mental health conditions more commonly known as mental illness. Like most people in society, I acknowledged that mental illness does exist, but remained in denial regarding the depth and severity of these illnesses. According to studies conducted by (The National Alliance on Mental Illness (NAMI), 1 in 4 persons is affected by Mental Illness. The more I study, the more I believe that statistic could be even greater, because many that are affected go unreported.

There is a book called the *Diagnostic and Statistical Manual of Mental Disorders* (DSM). There have been many versions of it published throughout the years. The latest version, as of 2019, is the DSM V. I do remember the DSM III and have noticed that the criteria for certain disorders have changed throughout the years. The book is published by the American Psychiatric Association. It is used as the standard book for evaluating and diagnosing mental health conditions.

As Dante was eventually given a diagnosis of Schizoaffective Disorder by the psychiatrists, I looked up the criteria for this disorder in the manual. According to the DSM IV, the diagnosis of Schizoaffective Disorder is just "plain confusing." There have been many interpretations in use for this confusing category, the book states. Throughout the years the interpretation has changed.

Currently, to be given a diagnosis of Schizoaffective Disorder, you must display a cross between a mood disorder and schizophrenia.

It is also characterized as a form of bipolar disorder. As you read on in the manual, the author states again that the diagnosis is confusing because some clinicians want to put the diagnosis in even another category, calling it a separate type of psychosis or simply a collection of confusing (used the word again) sometimes contradictory symptoms.

After reading all of this, I concluded that many clinicians are confused about the diagnosis, but Dante did meet the criteria of many of the bullet points that were used to formulate the diagnosis. I then began to feel that, even if the clinicians were not 100 percent correct, they were very close.

The book goes on to say that recent studies indicate that Schizoaffective Disorder patients who have predominant manic symptoms versus depressive symptoms have a better prognosis or outcome. I was relieved to read that as Dante had been given the diagnosis with manic symptoms and not depressive.

He is going to be okay, I thought to myself.

The book does indicate the symptoms needed to give one this disorder. For at least one month, the person must have 2 or more of the following:

1. Delusions (only one symptom is required if a delusion is reality bizarre i.e. being abducted by a spaceship from the sun).
2. Hallucinations (only one is required if 2 voices are talking to each other or one voice keeps up a running commentary on the persons thoughts or actions.
3. Speech that is incoherent or disorganized.
4. Disorganized or catatonic behavior- can't speak or move, stupor, rigidity or extreme excitement (babbling).
5. Any negative symptoms such as flat affect, reduced speech or lack of volition (your own will).

6. During the same time the person may have had a manic or depressed episode.

7. The disorder is not caused directly by a general medical condition or the use of substances, including prescription medications.

The book goes on to provide examples of people who have experienced these symptoms and how their diagnosis was determined. For the purposes of this book, however, I felt the need to tell Dante's story.

Chapter 3
The Day as I Saw It

Before further explaining how Dante ended up at a Forensic Institute, I want to retell the day of 'The Incident' as I saw the turn of events occur.

My recollection of events are as follows:

It was a fairly nice Sunday. The weather was just about perfect, not too cold and not too hot. I had gone to bed early the night before, which was not typical of me, but it was something that I felt that I needed to do in order to get up for the early morning church service at The First Cathedral. I had been a passive member of the church for about 10 years, and every Sunday I would make an unfulfilled promise that I would become more involved and join a ministry.

I became more serious about this promise after the death of one of my closest girlfriends, Sylvana. She would also make the same promise. We said that we would join something together. As she died suddenly of a diabetic coma, this sadly, never happened.

On this beautiful Sunday morning, Dante got up on his own, not typical of him, and said that he would be attending church with me, without me asking him to do so. This was so uncharacteristic of him that it should have been Clue Number One that something was not right. I, instead, was elated that he had got up on his own and ironed his white shirt with no prompting from me. In hindsight, as he got older, he would usually iron, so I can't say that that was a big surprise. Ever since 10th grade or so, good looks became the " in thing" to do.

We both then went to church. His sister had no desire to go on this morning and I, admittedly, did not push her. She was now 24 years old. My son felt the need to wear dark sunglasses to church. This should have been Clue Number Two, but I felt that he was just being a ridiculous teenager trying to look "cool." As we entered the church, I motioned him to take off the sunglasses and he insisted that it was part of his look for the day. This should have been Clue Number Three. Dante usually listened to me, especially the older he became. I am aware that this is opposite of many youths, but Dante seemed to become more cooperative the older he got.

Nevertheless, I did not argue much with him. We sat in church and he would take his sunglasses off but would then put them back on. Then, he just started fidgeting with them and looking around the church asking why the church seemed so empty this morning. That part was actually not a delusion; the church did appear more empty than usual. We were also on time for once and the members would usually stroll in as the service moved along.

By the time the Bishop started to preach his sermon, the congregation was a bit bigger. While the Bishop preached, Dante had difficulty sitting still and would giggle inappropriately, saying that the sermon was funny. He did say in the weeks to come that he felt the sermon that was preached that day spoke to him directly. The sermon was taken from the Book of Joshua.

Eventually, Dante excused himself and went outside to wait in the car. After church was over and we were headed home, I asked Dante what was so funny that he had to leave? He said, it was just funny and stared out of the window, another clue.

Once we returned home, Dante decided he needed to go to CVS again. I had just taken him once on the way home from church. Thus, began the turn of events that would forever change the lives of our family.

Chapter 4
The Phone Call

At approximately 3:00 pm on Sunday, September 28th, I received a call from the Bloomfield Police Department. An officer telephoned me saying, "I have good news and bad news. Which would you like to hear first?"

His tone was light, serious, but not extremely so. He decided to give me the good news first. He stated that the good news is that no one was hurt. The bad news is that they had my son at the Bloomfield Precinct. He was in a bit of trouble, but the officer's tone remained light. I did not think whatever occurred was extremely serious, and I told the officer that I would be there in a few minutes to pick Dante up.

The officer's tone then changed a bit, stating that it is not that simple.

"You cannot just come and pick him up. He will have charges against him and a bond will be set."

I asked about the charges and the officer proceeded to explain what had happened. I, in return, told the officer that my son has never committed a crime in his life and if he has been involved in such an incident, he must be psychotic. He had been previously diagnosed with bipolar disorder.

"He needs to get to the hospital," I said.

The officer said that he would talk to Dante about going to the hospital. He put me on hold for a few minutes and came back to the phone, stating that Dante did not want to go to the hospital. I informed the officer that he needed to go.

The officer convinced me that Dante would be alright staying in the precinct for one night. He would be brought to court the first thing in the morning. He advised me to be there by 9:00 a.m.

"Where," I asked.

He then gave me the address of a criminal court. The conversation ended.

I was numb after the call and in a state of shock. I informed my daughter who was at home. Neither of us thought that the incident was so serious that it would not simply be cleared up in the morning during court. Dante would then go to the hospital, get treated, and soon be back home. That was the routine we had become accustomed to whenever Big Dante would have a manic episode.

Chapter 5
The Hartford Court

Unlike Big Dante's manic episodes, Dante's now second psychotic episode had become criminal. My daughter and I went to the court with the expectation that everything would be cleared up that morning, and Dante would be ordered to go to the hospital. Instead, what occurred was nothing short of mind boggling and mind blowing.

Dante had an initial bail amount of $200,000 that was set by the Bloomfield, CT Police Department, which was unbeknownst to me until the morning of court. What occurred next was even more astonishing. As the Public Defender, who was automatically assigned to Dante, advocated to get the bail reduced to $75,000, the judge seemingly on a whim, decided the bail amount would instead now be $500,000!

"A half a million dollars," she said, and slammed the gavel down.

Dante was then taken away like a slave, in my mind. This was only the first of many times that he would be taken away in this manner. I found out immediately after the bail amount was given that the news media had gotten a hold of the incident and had sensationalized the story. The story had now gone viral throughout the state. Dante's mug-shot was front and center of the Newspaper's Crime section, and every news station was reporting on the incident stating that it was "Breaking News!"

Chapter 6
The Prison

Dante was initially taken to a holding cell and then to the correctional institute where they take everyone that is waiting to be charged with a crime. As did I, the Public Defender seemed in total shock over the bail amount that was given, and quickly instructed me to go to the Social Worker of the judicial court. She felt that he could be of some assistance.

My daughter and I went to find this person. He was not in his office, but we did run into him in the hallway as we were leaving. I told him that the Public Defender had suggested that we speak with him. I attempted to explain what had just happened in the courtroom, not completely understanding what had happened myself.

The Social Worker responded as if he knew the system was just corrupt and flawed, and he stated that he would see what he could do. He wrote Dante's name on a yellow Sticky Note, along with my cell phone number, and stated that he would give me a call as soon as he found something out.

As my daughter and I were leaving, reporters from various news channels swarmed around us with microphones trying to get a story. I almost spoke, but my daughter, who had just received her degree in Media Communications, nudged me saying the story wouldn't be the same once the media reported it. I did not say anything, but did take everyone's business card, including The Courant reporter who would go on to remain in our lives for the next two years after the incident.

My daughter and I drove home. We both had to take a day off from work, as neither of us knew if we were coming or going. Big Dante recently had his own manic episode and was already in the hospital trying to recover and put his life into perspective again. I wanted to call him and at least let him know what was going on. However, I decided to wait. I did not know if he could handle such news or how he would handle it. I needed to call the family. As my children, along with Big Dante, were my closest family in the area, except for Uncle John who lived closer by, I had to call out of state to reach everyone else.

We had not been in strong communication with Uncle John over the years, except for the routine family get-togethers on the holidays. After calling the family members, including Uncle John, and putting everyone in a frenzy, Big Dante called.

"Why do I keep hearing my name on the news," he asked. "What is going on?"

I attempted to tell the short of the story to Big Dante who had been stabilized by the *Haldol* that was given to him. He was able to handle the story and did not freak out. I told him that I was waiting to hear from a court Social Worker who was supposed to give me a call after he found something out. Big Dante stated that he wanted to know as soon as I heard anything further.

"Will do," I replied, and hung up the phone.

The next call I received was from Dante. He had been immediately placed in the mental health section of the correctional institute. The Social Worker on the unit called and said that my son would like to speak with me. Dante was clearly not himself. He was speaking very fast and did not know exactly where he was but said that he was okay.

The Social Worker took the phone and gave me a couple of numbers that I could call back on. He said that Dante would be given a cell, and they would constantly be checking in on him. He inquired regarding the types of medications Dante had been taking. I informed the worker that Dante had been discharged from the hospital with *Depakote* a couple of years prior but had been doing well without this medication until now.

From there, all I could do was wait. The following morning, the court Social Worker called, as promised. He said that he had gone to the jail to visit Dante. The Social Worker stated that Dante was in a state of complete acute psychosis. He had no idea where he was and wanted to come home with him.

"Poor thing," I vividly remember the Social Worker saying.

The Social Worker said that he was going to work on getting him moved to a youth jail, at least. I told the Social Worker that my family was discussing getting a private attorney to help us sort all of this out. He stated, if we do this, he could no longer be of assistance. He was going to try and see what services he could get.

His tone then changed; he sounded a bit more threatening.

"If you get an attorney, I can no longer help, so let me know what you are going to do," he said.

When I inquired regarding what services he could get, he once again said he cannot talk about it if we got an attorney, so let him know once we decide. He then hung up.

I just stood there looking at the phone, thinking *what just happened*? Why the sudden change when getting the private attorney was mentioned? The fact that the court Social Worker's tone changed so drastically, made me feel that I must get an attorney; something was not right.

My daughter felt that we should telephone the young attorney that we had seen on the elevator at the courthouse. She casually knew him from the Young Professionals' get togethers that she had been attending recently. Not even thinking about going on a massive search for a specific attorney, I decided to call him.

I felt that I needed someone quickly; someone who could explain that this had all been a big mistake and a mix up.

My son did not mean any harm to anyone and no physical harm was done to anyone, except for him. This should all be cleared up in no time, I thought. This should not be difficult for an attorney to explain, right?

Chapter 7
The Judicial System, and Attorney # 1

We telephoned the attorney. He sounded reasonable enough. I briefly explained what had happened. He stated that he had been in the courtroom when the case was being heard earlier that day. He didn't quite understand why the bond was so high, he said.

The case was getting media attention. Unfortunately, this oftentimes may affect the judge's judgement, he said.

"Well it shouldn't," I said. "How about racism? Could that have been the reason?"

"Could have been," he replied. "That's just the way it is. Once you are able to pay the retainer fee, I can begin my work."

We arranged to meet later that day. Family members came together to wire money for attorney fees. Since the bail amount was so high, the first order of business would be to get the bail amount lowered so that Dante could be released.

My daughter and I went to meet with the attorney. We gave him enough money to start his services. The attorney stated that he would go and visit Dante later that night, which he did. After the visit, the attorney telephoned to say that he had visited Dante and he remained "out of it." He was not able to really speak with him because Dante was not making much sense. He might need a psychologist or someone to go and assess him. He would telephone a psychologist that he knew and get back to me regarding what should be done next.

Meanwhile, at the correctional institution, Dante remained psychotic and in a manic state. The director of the correctional institute just happened to be a family friend. I had no idea that he had been promoted. He called and gave a few words of encouragement. He stated that Dante is "out of it," but he would check in on him as much as possible. Everything would be okay. Whether everything would actually be okay or not, no one really knew. However, his words were encouraging and pacifying for the moment.

The following morning, I received a call from Dante. A staff worker allowed him to call. He had been moved to a medical correctional facility, a regular prison where more services can be received if you are in a psychotic state, they said. Dante was still speaking fast, but he was coherent.

He said they took him on a long ride in a truck or something.

"I am in that town where the kid shot all of those children in the school last year. I think that they are going to try and pin those murders on me," he said.

He was no longer completely psychotic, but he was confused and knew that he was in quite a bit of trouble. He attempted to tell me about the incident that occurred on that Sunday that landed him in jail. He did remember the events of the day prior to the incident. The staffer interrupted and said that Dante had to now hang up, but not before he gave me the name of some hip-hop artist that he thought may be able to help bail him out of jail. I told Dante that I, as well as the family, would do all that we could to get him out of there and hung up.

I immediately telephoned the attorney to inform him that Dante had been moved somewhere further away. He said that he would go there to visit. I then telephoned the director of the correctional institute that he had been moved away from. He said that a judgement call was made overnight, and when he arrived that morning, the van was already *en route*. The prison where they transported him to would better be able to assist him, he said. It was supposed to have more resources.

Dante was able to telephone again and describe his new surroundings. He stated that the facility was much cleaner than the first facility. He was in a cell by himself, and on a constant watch. He was on a unit where they considered him to be very unstable. Even though Dante described the environment as awful, I knew just from visiting prisons in my own work as a Case Manager that his environment could have been much worse. He was able to have a cell to himself the entire time that he had to stay there. My biggest fear was his contact with the wrong person or people, and the possibility that physical and/or mental harm could occur.

Chapter 8
More Court

Dante went back and forth to court a few times after that. One court date was held without our family or attorney's knowledge.

"They do that sometimes," the attorney said, "even though we try to stop them."

The attorney often spoke in terms of "they." I eventually asked him who are the "they" people that he keeps speaking of?

"Some of the decision makers," he said.

I wanted to challenge these decisions makers, but with all the trouble that we were already in, I felt it was best to save that battle for another day.

The few times that Dante was brought back and forth from the correctional facility to court were for what the court called continuances. A decision was not made regarding reducing the bail or the charges, so Dante was brought back to the correctional facility. These were the only times that the family was allowed to see Dante.

He was in a prison uniform. His was blue instead of that standard orange that I had seen in my work with inmates. He was thin. Uncle John, who attended every court date since he got the call, felt that Dante was unrecognizably thin. He seemed to be getting used to wearing handcuffs. One time, he even gave the family a wave, handcuffs on and all.

During the time that Dante was in jail, I connected with as many politicians and community leaders that I could think of to inform them of what had happened. I had met quite a few leaders in my travels of work as Employment Coordinator and my community work as a Board Secretary for our local Civic Association.

I met with the Police Chief first and attempted to explain what had happened. He was very empathetic and said that he had not heard the story that went viral in the media, even though it was his department that had raised the charges. He said that he would try to help as much as he could, and he did try.

His staffer called the very next morning. His portion of the bail was dropped. Since there was another police department involved, I needed to connect with that Police Chief as well. Unfortunately, I didn't know him.

In hindsight, I still could have tried harder to connect with him. The lesson reinforced and reiterated throughout this entire case was that it is all about who you know and who knows you and how far they would be willing to go to help, or if they even really had the power to do so.

I continued to meet with leaders, both local and even some state political figures, trying to get them to understand that this was all a sensationalized mistake. Yes, my son had gotten himself into a mess, but he did not commit an intentional crime, I would continue to tell them. Most of the leaders were empathetic to the story, but none of them were really sure what, if anything, they could do.

Chapter 9
The Release

I decided that I would get back to meeting with the political leaders later. I did not have time to waste. The longer Dante stayed in that awful jail, the more potential there was for something bad to eventually happen.

I telephoned the attorney.

"What is the plan?" I asked.

Dante needed to get out of that prison on his next court date, not to mention that he would be turning 19 years old the same day the next court date was scheduled. I told the attorney this with a tone of impatient frustration. The attorney responded that Dante had been examined for competency and the results came back inconclusive. He was neither competent nor incompetent.

"I will try to convince the judge to lower the bail so that we can get him out," he said.

He tried to pacify me.

"Do you think that you can do it?" I asked with nervous anxiety.

"We should be able to," he responded, trying to reassure me so that I would calm down. From his tone, I could tell that he was unsure.

On the day of court, a few family members gathered. Prayers were said, and we went into the courtroom, not sure of what to expect. The defense, our attorney, stated what we desired to happen, and the prosecution countered. The judge read the competency report that had been given to her and she did not know what to think or do.

As she appeared to be stuck, she said, "bail denied," and reordered the exam. I became extremely uncharacteristically frustrated and verbally questioned the judge's intelligence, apparently louder than I thought, and was warned that I would be asked to leave. As court was over anyways, there would be no need to escort me out. I left. The entire family left. My daughter had already left as the whole situation had already made her physically sick and she went to the bathroom to throw up.

I went to find the bondsman. The bondsman had already spoken with me on previous court dates of ways to possibly get Dante released. I found the bondsman and told him that we would get the money. He gave us an arrangement, and we went to get the money.

When the judge heard that our family had come up with the money, she felt that criminal activity must have been involved, like drug dealing or something. How else could black people legally come up with so much money so fast, she must have thought.

The bondsman went to pay the bond. Dante, luckily, was still in the holding cell waiting for the other prisoners to complete their court cases. Afterwards, the bondsman ran around the courthouse like a chicken with his head cut off, trying to make arrangements to release Dante. They finally brought him back upstairs from the holding cell. There was talk that he may have to be transported to another jail before he could be finally released.

Within an hour, that plan changed. The judge then decided that she could not release Dante without putting a "slave bracelet" on his ankle. The bracelet is actually a monitoring or tracking device. It reminded me of the shackles that I had seen in the movies about slavery, so I just felt that it was only appropriate to refer to it as a "slave bracelet."

The judge called Dante up from the holding cell and spoke to him as if he were not psychotic and just another young, black male that needed to be criminalized, locked up, and given a criminal record. She told him that she would let him go home with the monitor, and that he cannot stop by McDonald's on the way home. She then left.

The bondsman was prepared to set up the bail transaction when a call suddenly came from the "medical prison" were Dante had been incarcerated. The Discharge Planner of the prison said that he had no idea that there was a plan for discharge and he needed to get Dante medically approved. I was then given the phone to speak with the Prison Discharge Planner.

"I had no idea that there was a plan for his discharge," he said.

I again became uncharacteristically frustrated. I told the Discharge Planner in the calmest voice that I could feign:

"I have been telling the staff there for a couple of weeks that on Dante's next court date, I am getting him out of there before you guys kill him with the wrong medications."

Dante was never stabilized while in the "medical prison."

The bail remained at half a million dollars. It was actually fifty thousand more than that, but a portion was dropped due to my conversation with the Police Chief. The family paid a percentage of that, and Dante was eventually released on a Physician's Emergency Certificate. The release did not come before bouts of back and forth speaking with the Prison Discharge Planner about properly discharging Dante. He argued that there may not be a bed to place Dante in at the hospital. As I did have some experience with the hospital from dealing with Big Dante's admissions and discharges, I knew if the insurance was right, they would take Dante. For once in my life, I had good health insurance. And just as I thought, when they saw the insurance card, they found a bed for Dante.

The court staffers continuously apologized for Dante not being able to go directly home. I informed the seemingly well-intentioned staffers that Dante needed to go to the hospital and if they did not release him to a hospital, I would be taking him there anyway. No one was able to see that he was still psychotic. All that they could see is just another young, black male. Whether my thinking was right or wrong, this is how I felt.

An ambulance was called to transport Dante to the hospital. Our family waited in the courthouse if we could for the ambulance to arrive. Some family members had to leave, as it was getting late and the courthouse was closing. The attorney had left long ago and didn't even know the family's back-up plan. The judge was also gone.

The guards needed to leave and lock up. They asked our family to wait in the parking garage. The ambulance would be arriving there, a guard said. Our family went to the indoor garage that was under the courthouse. We waited, and waited, and waited. The sun set, and the moon began to shine through openings in the rooftop.

A lady from the Psychological Medical Center showed up from out of nowhere and came walking through the garage. She had the Physicians Emergency Certificate (PEC) and I had to sign some sort of release stating which hospital Dante should go to. Eventually, the ambulance came. The guard, who I assumed had to work overtime to wait for the ambulance, brought Dante out. He was transported to the local hospital.

Dante was extremely happy to see his family. He was still a bit manic but more coherent than I thought he would be. The prison staffers had described a totally psychotic young man. It was only for this reason that I concluded that the judge may not have been able to detect his continued psychotic state when she spoke with him earlier that day.

As the saying goes, "you have to know the man that has the illness." In order to detect such things, you would have had to really know more about him and his personality.

He was in psychosis the entire day of the "crime" and I did not know it. I have since become an intellect and advocate of knowing the warning signs of psychosis in great detail. Without research, awareness and knowledge, it can be hard to know. Even then, it can still be difficult, the more education and knowledge, the better.

Chapter 10
Institute of Living

Dante was admitted for observation for one day to the local hospital. The following day, he was immediately transferred to the Institute of Living for stabilization.

The experience of the Institute of Living was nothing short of a time filled with uncertainty for the family and a feeling of *what will happen next?* The staff of the institute stabilized Dante within two weeks of the psychiatric hospital stay. The family visited Dante every day during this time to check on his wellbeing and note his progress. The family would bring board games and card games to play with the hopes of experiencing a more cheerful visit. Depending on Dante's mood, he would choose to play or not play the board games.

As insurance appears to drive patient's length of stay, patients today usually do not stay for more than two weeks in this facility. This was the case with Dante. The clinical team of the Institute felt that the correct medication had been prescribed and dispensed. The Psychiatrist discharged Dante with a discharge note. The note gave follow up instructions.

> *Continue to take medications as prescribed and follow up with the outpatient program Community Health Resources (CHR).*

> Addendum:

> *Follow the instructions of the court.*

Chapter 11
The First Discharge

In December 2014, Dante was discharged from The Institute of Living. As he had been incarcerated for 6 weeks prior to the hospitalization, his hair was an utter mess. He had always liked going to the barber shop. It had been a long time since he had his last haircut, so he was anxious to go. Prior to the incident, I had been critical of his bi-weekly and sometimes weekly haircut schedule, but on this day, I was anxious for him to get a haircut.

Dante had been assigned a Probation Officer before entering the hospital. The Probation Officer initially stated that cases like Dante's are more difficult for him to deal with. In these cases, the guys are not considered criminals but mental health cases, they are often still treated as criminals, so it gets confusing, he admitted. As this Probation Officer, Chuck, had been calling for the entire two weeks that Dante was in the hospital, I felt that I should call him and inform him that Dante had now been discharged. I called the officer, informed him that Dante had been released, and that he badly needed a haircut. The Probation Officer seemed friendly enough and said after getting Dante's haircut, he would need to come to the probation office so that next steps could be discussed. I informed the Probation Officer that I would bring Dante to him afterwards.

Dante got his haircut by his regular barber who had been taking care of his hair since he was 9 years old. While cutting his hair, the barber asked Dante to explain to him his version of what had occurred on the day in question and the day that the media sensationalized and defamed Dante's name all over the State and down the east coast to the Washington Post newspaper. As Dante attempted to explain what had happened, I realized that he was not completely stabilized. If he was stabilized, he sincerely felt that God had commanded him to behave the way that he did on that Sunday that changed his whole life, the day that made the breaking news media story of the night for whatever reason.

Nevertheless, Dante got his haircut. Afterwards, we made a couple of stops while *en route* to the probation office. Dante's paternal grandmother ironically passed away a week before Dante's discharge, and the family was gathering for the burial. The funeral had taken place earlier that day. I had attended the funeral just prior to picking Dante up from the hospital. I took him to pay his respects to the family, and then headed downtown to the probation office.

Chapter 12
The Probation Officer

The Probation Officer met Dante on this day and explained to him and to me as well that he had been ordered to place a monitoring bracelet on his ankle. The whole notion of bracelet and chains was just so reminiscent of the slavery system, to me, but I continued to listen.

The Probation Officer said that he would have to send the technician out to the home to have the bracelet connected. The Probation Officer proceeded to call to order the bracelet. Dante's name was no longer in the system to have a bracelet. If I knew then what I know now, I would have tried to stop this process. There was a reason Dante's name was no longer in the system; it should have been questioned and investigated further. The Probation Officer had to reorder the monitoring bracelet and set a time for the technician to come to the home and set the system up.

As it was decided that Dante would temporarily reside with our Uncle John, the system was ordered for set up in his home. Dante and I headed to our home to pack his things for at least a month and then headed to Uncle John's home.

Uncle John had an upstairs room for Dante, which ironically, overlooked the graveyard where the "crime" had occurred. I was concerned about that at first, but as Dante was now more stabilized, the connection to the graveyard appeared to have no real significance. Dante brought his PlayStation 4. As long as he had that, he was in his comfort zone.

The technician arrived later that evening with the monitor bracelet and a box that looked like a cable box. I found the whole set up really interesting. A "slave bracelet" that is supposed to track your whereabouts. I thought about my work with formerly incarcerated men. I thought about the day two white guys escaped from a Connecticut prison. All of the guys on my caseload, who formerly wore "ankle monitors" were called by their probation officers, all at the same time to report back to the officers to have the bracelets placed back on their ankles. Re-punished for someone else's wrongdoing, I remember thinking to myself. The day the guys were called, they were in a training program to try and better their lives. I remember the class being full, and then, suddenly it was empty.

I was now feeling and going through some of their experiences via watching this madness occur to my son. I felt for the guys the day that it happened. It just became even more real since it was now happening in my immediate family.

The technician put the bracelet on with no emotion. He didn't say much; he may have asked if the bracelet was too tight. When Dante said no, the technician said, "ok" and left. We would later find out that the bracelet was not connected properly. It took about two weeks for staff to realize the monitor was not recording. If Dante was "that guy," he could have traveled to another country in that amount of time. Fortunately, Dante was not that guy and actually not even a criminal but had been criminalized, nevertheless.

Dante would go on to visit the Probation Officer weekly and give urine samples, even though he never used drugs. What a waste of taxpayers' dollars, I thought to myself.

The Probation Officer would often comment on Dante being a good kid. On occasions, he would forego drug testing. He would also continue to comment that mental health cases are some of his hardest cases. As he had said that a couple of times, I realized more training was obviously needed on these issues for probation officers and the entire judicial system.

Chapter 13
Uncle John

The family decided that Dante would temporarily reside with Uncle John until we could all get a better understanding of the court process. Uncle John became very instrumental in helping all of us deal with this unforeseen situation. Uncle John is actually our cousin, but he was raised in the South along with my dad like his brother, so he is more like an uncle. Uncle John would share stories for days about the racism he and my dad experienced throughout their lifetimes and has vowed to write a book of his own about his vast experiences. Uncle John agreed that having Dante reside with him would be a good idea as he was now retired and able to help. So, we packed Dante's clothes and traveled just a couple of miles away to Uncle John's.

Dante stayed with Uncle John throughout the holiday season of 2014. This season would be a time of stabilization for Dante and the rest of the family, including Big Dante who had been just recently discharged from his own hospital stay. Dante took the medication that had been prescribed to him daily and appeared to become mentally stronger with each passing day. The "slave bracelet" had been secured on his ankle by the technician. The monitoring device was supposed to monitor Dante's every move. The curfew that was initially court ordered stated that Dante had to stay indoors 24/7 hours. Again, in hindsight, as Dante became stabilized, our attorney should have requested reconsideration of the order.

The attorney did say that we would have to go back to court to get permission for Dante to attend his outpatient programming with the Community Health Resources (CHR) program. A court date was quickly set for Dante to attend this programming. In December 2014, Dante and the attorney went before Judge Noel to get permission for Dante to attend his outpatient program. Judge

White, the more unreasonable judge, was away on vacation this particular morning. As our attorney stated the case, the reasonable Judge, Judge Noel easily decided that Dante should be allowed to attend his outpatient program. The attorney also requested the judge grant permission for Dante to visit his law office for continued counsel. Judge Noel easily granted both requests.

I wonder to this day what would have occurred if Judge White were not on vacation and the attorney had to plead the case to her instead. Would she have been as understanding? It was meant to happen the way it happened, I have concluded. And so, it was, the 24/7 house arrest was lifted for these situations only. Since Dante did not have a criminal mind, it was easy for him to abide by the orders that had been given to him. He appeared to take the situation one day at a time and continued to heal.

The court system appeared to see Dante as only a young black male. No matter what kind of individual person he might be, he would be viewed as a stereotypical criminal.

The stereotype of young black men is so deep rooted and intertwined into the fabric of society that there is no way Dante could possibly be a young man who was actually doing well in society, going to community college, working, and paying taxes like a good citizen should do. And young black males definitely do not have mental health disorders. He had to be a criminal. They all have to be criminals. This message became consistent and more apparent as the case moved along.

Uncle John became the person who would get Dante to all of his outpatient appointments on time. Dante was put on what the courts called a pre-trial probation; he would visit Chuck, the Probation Officer, for weekly appointments. During these appointments, Dante would continue to give a urine specimen; the drug tests were clean each week. The probation officer eventually began to drug test every other week. Maybe he began to realize that drug testing was a waste of tax payers' money. And so, it went. This became our way of life for the next 12 months.

Chapter 14
The End of Attorney # 1

As our attorney continued to attempt to work on Dante's case, the family became somewhat frustrated with the pace of the case, and the fact that the attorney was not able to answer questions with clarity regarding the future outcome of the case. Again, in hindsight, it appears that attorneys in general have difficulty with direct transparency. It may be a lawyer thing, or it may be the inconsistencies and the unpredictably of the court system. I would like to believe that it is more the latter.

It was a difficult thing to do, but as I had the most communication with the attorney, I needed to be the one to inform the attorney that the family had chosen alternate counsel. I was more conflicted about the decision to seek alternate counsel than some of my family members. The attorney did fight to get the "murder bond" reduced from $ 500,000 to $100,000, even though the fight was unsuccessful. Judge White appeared to be swayed by all of the media coverage and attention, not to mention the young, black male stereotype. Judge White also appeared to have difficulty understanding Dante's mental health diagnosis, or she just did not care nor want to understand. I have a vivid memory of the judge rolling her eyes sideways and into the air as she ordered Dante to the corrections facility and told the officers to place him on the mental health unit as if to say, whatever.

Our attorney also attended Dante's psychological evaluation after it was ordered for the second time when the first evaluation came back inconclusive. The attorney did sit with Dante throughout the entire two-hour evaluation. Dante did feel comfortable with this attorney, but the family felt that the attorney needed a stronger plan. Up until this point, the attorney did not seem to have a concrete plan for the direction of the case.

It was only through talking to others that were familiar with the court system and criminal cases that I found out about the first-time offenders Diversion Program. I mentioned the program to the attorney. The attorney stated that he thought that the initial charges given to Dante were too serious for the Diversion Program, but when he revisited the charges, he realized that Dante did qualify for the program. The charges listed were not as severe as he thought. Unfortunately, by this time the family had already been in discussions with potential attorney #2 and decided to pursue the Diversion Program with the new attorney.

Chapter 15
Attorney # 2

The initial discussions with Attorney #2, Attorney Blue, began during the holiday season of 2014. This attorney's name had been given to me by someone at the court. Again, in hindsight, this should have been a clue of how this relationship may run its course. I telephoned the attorney to discuss the background of Dante's case. The attorney assured me that he had a good relationship with the judge and would be able to "make things happen." He did not want to make any guarantees, which appears to be universal lawyer talk. As the entire family was in town for the holidays, I set up an appointment so that the attorney could meet all of us at once.

In between Christmas and New Year's Eve, Attorney Blue met with Dante, me, Uncle John, Dante's grandparents, Big Dante, Dante's sister, his uncle Calvin and other family members of interest. The Attorney was not expecting such a turnout and moved the meeting to one of his bigger libraries. Attorney Blue's office was not as modernized as our first attorney's. Attorney Blue's office had a more vintage feel to it. Attorney #1's office had marble floors and a remote-controlled fire place, amongst many other modern-day amenities. Attorney #1 was also a young black man, scarcely 30 years old. Attorney Blue was an older white Jewish male.

Dante had been stabilized and was able to verbalize his opinions and feelings regarding the direction of the case. He was now very much like his old self. Attorney Blue directed the initial question to Dante. He inquired of Dante to tell a little about himself, the old interview question. Dante proceeded to talk about his school life and present family situation and recent work history including his job at Wal Mart. The Attorney then inquired of Dante to tell in his own words what happened on the day in question. Dante proceeded to do so to the best of his ability, without taking too much time to do so. This was the first time the family had heard the story in its entirety from Dante's point of view. Up until this point, everyone else had been trying to explain what had happened to the courts. I am not sure why we were trying to speak for Dante. Even though he was in psychosis on the day in question, he appeared to remember very well what had happened.

Dante explained his side of the story and Attorney Blue stated that he would have to think for a few days regarding the best way to approach the case. He did state at this very first meeting that a plea deal may be needed. He also stated that he could manipulate the charges and at least try for probation. I was not in agreement with any of the suggestions, as they all included Dante having a criminal record. It was difficult for me to get past the notion, if there was no criminal intent and no one was hurt, why should Dante be given a criminal record that would ruin his life for at the least a very long time, if not forever? The Attorney did state that Dante may have to have a criminal record for some time, but it could eventually get expunged. I could only think about the men that I had worked with in my field of work who had criminal records. I had extreme difficulty assisting them with obtaining employment. The darker your skin tone, the more difficult it became to assist with the employment search. Adding a criminal record just made it even worse.

As Dante is of a darker hue, even though handsome, skin color would still supersede being handsome. We are living in the "looks are everything" generation, more so than ever. Handsome is nice, but color would continue to play a factor.

I motioned the attorney to consider the Diversion Program. He did not appear to be too familiar with it. I had already Googled it and printed it off. He asked me for a copy. He made a copy and decided to get back to the family on how we should proceed with the court case, but for now he would just ask the judge for a continuance.

Chapter 16
Court Continues

And so it went. The year 2015 began a different way of life for our entire family. We had become a part of the ridiculous, corrupt, Judicial System, the system that I had grown accustomed to only by listening to guys on my caseload, all of whom had criminal records. They would tell me horror stories about the racist judges, the prosecutors, and other officers within the system. I was not ignorant to what was going on within the judicial system, but on second thought, maybe I was. Dante's case seemed so cut and dry to me. How did the process spiral so out of control? I was not minimizing what had occurred, but had it not been for a mental psychotic episode, the entire incident or " crime" would not have occurred.

I did continue to say that no one was hurt (except Dante), and that he was not trying to steal anyone's car. He had his own 2007 Black Maxima sitting in the driveway on the day in question. There was no intent and no motive. He was not trying to be a part of a gang initiation and was not even hanging out with a group of his boys. Peer pressure was not even the issue. It was purely a psychotic episode, a situation that could be rectified with therapy and medication. The family who were considered the victims were not pressing any charges. They never even came to court. They obviously realized that no harm was done. The victims were able to assault Dante and bruise his face and body to retaliate and receive no repercussions. Maybe they considered the score even? The court system, however, decided the case could not possibly have a simple solution. It was sensationalized in the media. Dante must be punished.

In January 2015, Attorney Blue asked for a continuance. Uncle John brought Dante to court on this morning and I took a half day off work. This became a usual pattern throughout the year. I would take a half a day off from my government job to attend court dates and therapy sessions for Dante's case. I am inclined to say, only in the State of Connecticut would such a waste of time occur, but as I study cases all around the country, the Criminal Justice system has a serious problem throughout the nation. The common denominator appears to be money. Why the system wants to exploit others for financial gain is a story in and of itself.

During the month of February 2015, Attorney Blue did submit the paperwork to request the Diversion Program for Dante. He worked on a nice proposal explaining why Dante should be granted the Diversion Program. Judge White ordered Dante to be assessed by the clinicians that worked with the court in order to receive the Diversion Program.

The Diversion Program is a mental health program for first time offenders with a mental health condition. Dante met the basic requirements for the program. During this court session, the judge ordered the assessment and stated that a date would be given for the assessment; court then ended.

I turned to the attorney and asked, "now what?" He stated that he had another case, but that we should go downstairs to get a date for the assessment. I, along with Dante and Uncle John, blindly went downstairs looking for an appointment room for the assessment. After asking a couple of staff members if they knew where the appointment room was, the staffers also blindly walked around and tried to assist with finding the appointment room. Eventually, a staff member was able to point us in the right direction. This only occurred after explaining to staff member after staff member what had just taken place in the courtroom.

I asked the appointment lady for an appointment, but also had to explain again to her what had just occurred in the courtroom before she was able to figure out what type of appointment was needed. The appointment lady took my number and stated that someone would be calling with a time and date for the appointment.

Of course, no one called. We waited for over a week. Luckily, I had taken the appointment lady's number. I telephoned her back. I let her know that no one had called. She seemed surprised and put me hold. She stated that she just called the assessment office directly. They gave her a time and date to bring Dante in for an assessment. She gave me the information, and I wrote it in the calendar along with my many other appointments that were scheduled. Some appointments were directly for me, and some were for Dante.

Chapter 17
Dad's Sudden Death

In all the chaos of dealing with the court system and trying to explain mental illness and mental health conditions to those who pretended to or maybe really did not understand, I got a call from my mom.

"Your dad has been rushed to the hospital," she said.

Dad was a fairly healthy man at the now age of 79. I was concerned about the call, but not as concerned as I should have been. He had just been playing basketball a few months before with Dante. About an hour and a half later, I got another call from mom.

"Your dad is gone."

I initially wanted to think "gone where?" but I knew what she meant. I was just frozen at the stop sign where I had stopped driving to take the call. I didn't know what to say or think. What happened? is all I could think to say. Mom went on to explain how suddenly his death occurred. It was very quick. She was also in shock and told me that he always said he wanted to pass away with no pain or struggle and that is what happened. We both cried, and I told her that I would call back after sifting through what I needed to do next.

As mom and dad lived down South, we needed to get there. I drove home to try and gather my thoughts. I told Dante and his sister what had happened. Everyone remained in shock, but we knew that we needed to get south as soon as possible. We made plane reservations. Luckily, we had the money to do so, as this had not always been the case.

But then, there was the court and the issue of the "slave bracelet" that remained on Dante's ankle. I telephoned Attorney Blue to see what he could do. Initially, the attorney thought we would have to go back to court to get an order of permission. He called later that day and said that he spoke to Judge White and she said the bracelet could be removed so that he could go to the funeral. I was thinking, she must have taken her "happy pills" that day. That was the easiest request she had ever granted since the case began. I guess it was okay to be a danger down South as long as he was not in Connecticut. Nevertheless, I was thankful for her reasonableness on this day.

The Probation Officer told Dante to come to his office so that he could take the bracelet off. I transported him to the probation office and the officer took a pair of paper scissors and cut the bracelet off. It seemed like such a simple thing to do. The Probation Officer smiled after cutting it off, as if he felt Dante did not need it anyways. At this point, he did not need the bracelet on. He had been stabilized after leaving the hospital and was consistently taking his medication.

The very next day, we were all on a plane to Florida to try and get a grip on what had just occurred, to console mom, and to help prepare for dad's funeral. My brother Calvin was already there. He had already started with the preparations. He and his wife had begun to devise a very nice program with lots of family pictures. We called as many people as we could. Within a few days, a funeral was planned. A very nice one, if funerals could be labeled as such. It was a homegoing celebration, as this has become the term used by many in the Christian community, especially the African American community. It is the end of life as we know it. After life on earth, as long as you are saved, you will live in peace forever with the Lord in heaven.

The thought of dad living in peace was a consoling feeling for me. I felt that he would be alright. It was those of us that are still in the land of the living that had to now figure out how to move on without him.

Dad was a military man, so the service was eventful with

American flag tribute ceremony. There were at least 500 people at the funeral. Family traveled from all over to pay their respects. Mom held up really well, but probably mostly because she was still in a state of shock. Dante, along with his other first cousins was one of the pallbearers and carried the casket to the burial grounds. At the viewing, Cousin Karen, Uncle John's daughter presided. Family who could make it in for the Friday evening service from New York, Connecticut, and Georgia came to pay their respects.

As family members, friends, church friends and neighbors spoke and shared experiences, I got up as well to share my love for Dad. I could barely hold it together but tried to share how much he meant. Dante also got up and spoke. Over the last few years, he had gotten more comfortable with speaking in front of an audience as he aspired to be a musical performer/Hip Hop artist and had performed in front of crowds in talent shows and the like. Dante got up and shared how much his grandad meant to him, from helping with his math homework and encouraging him to study over the years to the last time had seen him a few months before. He had been surprised at how spry he was as they played basketball, for what he jokingly said for an "old man." Even in the midst of everything going on back in Connecticut, this was a ray of warmth in our sorrow over this loss. With proper medication, Dante was Dante, and if we could get the legal justice system to see this...

The day ended with the immediate family coming back to mom's house for the repast dinner. It was a sad occasion, but like a family reunion all at once.

Chapter 18
The Slave Bracelet Again

As life was still happening in Connecticut, Dante, his sister, and I stayed for a few days after the funeral and then had to head back to Connecticut. We immediately had to report to the Probation Officer that we were back in the area.

Dante and I reported to the probation office the first thing in the morning after returning from Florida. The Probation Officer called the courts to find out if it was alright for Dante to leave the monitoring bracelet off. Whomever he spoke to said, no. It may have been someone speaking for the judge or it may have been someone else; we may never know that one. In any case, the technician was ordered back to the house. He once again put the "slave bracelet" on. The technician was a black man who apologized for the system as he put the bracelet on. It felt like Dante was free for about a week and then sold back into slavery. Dante appeared to just accept all that was happening to him in stride. He remained totally calm from the day he initially left the hospital.

I was the one who had become very angry and tried to strategically figure out the most diplomatic way to fight this case without making things worse. I had already begun to feel that the case had become somewhat personal because Dante was bailed out from the ridiculous murder bond that was given in the beginning of the case. I continued to question why the dire need to lock someone up that does not need to be?

It had to be money.

Chapter 19
Diversion Program Denied

The scheduled date for Dante's assessment for the Diversion Program was shortly after dad's funeral. We traveled to a local mental health and rehab clinic. The Licensed Clinical Social Worker was nice enough and appeared to know what she was doing. She assessed Dante for a few hours and in her assessment wrote that Dante qualified for the Diversion Program. The clinical worker felt that he should continue with his current outpatient program and have the charges nullified once he completes the program. The final decision would be up to the judge, but usually the judge grants the program after the assessment states that one is qualified, she said.

A few weeks after the assessment was completed, another court session was held. Attorney Blue had written a very insightful report to include an explanation of mental health conditions and diagnoses. For whatever reason, Judge White did not receive the clinical assessment until just before Dante was called to appear in front of her. The judge read the assessment at this very moment for the very first time. She stated that the assessment states that Dante qualifies for the program. The judge looked over at the prosecutor. The prosecutor did not feel that Dante should be granted the Diversion Program. He had no concrete reason.

The story had been sensationalized in the media; that was the biggest reason that I could think of. The prosecutor nor the judge had never even heard the total story at this point. They could only be basing their assumptions and conclusions on the media story, and the one-sided story of the family who never made it to court. A formal investigation was never conducted, even though I had asked our first attorney about the investigation. Again, in hindsight, it appears that a formal investigation would have cost more money. Maybe that is why it was never done? In the transition between the two attorneys, the notion of the investigation was lost. I would have had to push the attorneys to request an investigation, and since I didn't, in all the chaos, a complete investigation was never conducted. Investigation or no investigation, the State of Connecticut felt it was their duty to keep this case going for as long as possible.

The Sandy Hook massacre that had occurred a few years back may have even had something to do with the treatment of Dante. The buzz was that the state had become even more conservative since the kid that killed the 26 students had been diagnosed with a mental illness. Why he was allowed to have guns with a known mental illness continues to bewilder me. I will save that discussion for another book, but I do have to distinguish these situations. Dante did not hurt anyone, there was no premeditation involved, and he definitely did not have any weapons.

The cases are no comparison. I do wonder how Adam's (that was the kid's name), case would have been tried if he had lived. After all, he was white. There are enough examples of blatant disparities of treatment in the judicial system based on race. If one doesn't know it, I am here to tell you. Just from our situation alone, I can reaffirm that there is. If Dante had blonde hair and blue eyes, our case would have ended with the Diversion Program.

Even though the laws are written stating that all should receive equal justice under the law, the stereotypes and wounds of yesteryear are too interwoven and intertwined into the fabric of society for this to occur. This must just stop. But it is obviously going to take many, many more discussions on race relations for equal justice to occur as it should for everyone.

The prosecutor was easily able to convince the judge that the charges were too serious to grant the Diversion Program. Even though, according to the law, the charges were in the guidelines of the program, but so it went. Program denied.

The denial of the program was a big disappointment on this day. I went back to work only to leave early. All of the events of the past month were just too much handle. Now, what are we going to do? The court case was supposed to have ended on this day, at least for a while.

Chapter 20
The Media

The media felt the need to write another article in the newspaper about the denial of the Diversion Program. It was "Breaking News," according to them. " Teen Denied Probation," the reporter wrote. The reporter, Ralph, wrote for the statewide newspaper, which also gets national attention. This reporter had become the lead reporter on the case. He would show up to all of Dante's court sessions and then write about the outcome that evening. The story was usually printed the following day in the morning newspaper. Freedom of the Press is what this intrusion was considered.

Other local newspapers would follow suit and take what the lead reporter had written and print the same story in their local newspaper. Sometimes, they would change the story around a bit. They did not copy the story verbatim. This appeared to be an even bigger problem. A few newspapers would use a few key words in their articles, and then they would just make the rest of the story up. One local newspaper reported that Dante had killed a10-year-old little girl, when in actuality, they should have reported that the little girl was checked out at the hospital and released with no injuries!

I did speak with the lead reporter on numerous occasions. I felt that his coverage of the case was getting better. After his write up of the Diversion Program denial, I felt the need to call him again. I needed to let him know that the correct name for the Diversion Program was the "Diversion Program," not probation as he had written. Again, in retrospect, I guess that it could be considered a probation program, but that was not the name of the program and I felt that the program's name had some significance.

The reporter was always cordial on the phone and even appeared apologetic, stating that his intent is to report the news correctly. I shared with Ralph that many family and friends have stated that Dante was tried in the media due to the sensationalized media coverage of the day in question. Reporter Ralph did not want to believe that. He stated that the media does not influence the decision making of the courts. With that, I just say okay, and I will write the next chapter.

Chapter 21
Now What?

After the judge denied the Diversion Program, I felt stuck and lost. The family was hoping that the Diversion Program would almost end the case. We knew that Dante would complete the program successfully, if he had been allowed to do so. He was already working the program and doing well with it. The judge decided not to recognize his accomplishments within the program. Even though the judge did not want to recognize the program as the evaluator suggested, Dante continued with the program.

Dante continued his counseling sessions with his therapist and clinical team. He participated in all the activities that were offered to him from the program. He was able to meet other youth that were his age who had been diagnosed with a mental health condition or mental illness. They would take them on day trips for exploration, museums, and the like. There was a youth advisory board that Dante became a part of and he was assigned a case manager to assist him with his job search. Dante also studied to obtain his driver's license and went to driving school. He passed the test and obtained his license. The program also assisted him with this.

As a parent, I can honestly say that I had no complaints about this mental health program. There should be more like it. That is my only complaint. Only in our many systems in Connecticut would we somehow drop the ball and not recognize the programs that are working.

As Dante continued to make progress with this mental health and youth program, I needed to figure out what should be done about this case that continued to hang around and over our lives like a bad dream. I wanted Attorney Blue to ask the judge to reconsider her decision regarding the Diversion Program. Attorney Blue said that he didn't want to try for fear of another rejection. He wanted to begin working on other deals. Other deals would give Dante a criminal record. In my mind, this was not an option.

As I was speaking with my Social Worker friend, Angie, during lunch one day, she suggested I try one more attorney. "He does not lose," she said. I telephoned this attorney and gave him the synopsis of the story and case. He was another young black attorney. He had a very confident tone.

"I can fix it," he said. "We can go back to the judge and get her to reconsider. Of course, money would be needed first, but I will fix it."

I met with this attorney a few days afterwards. He was young and handsome, and spoke with a confident tone, an "I can do anything" tone. Our first black attorney was about the same age and they appeared to run in similar circles. Our first attorney was just a bit more arrogant. Our first attorney would later find himself in federal prison for a white-collar crime. I will not dwell on this for the purposes of our story.

I discussed the retainer fee with our soon to be new attorney, Attorney Raheim. We discussed the actions that he was planning to take. Coincidentally, the young attorney was a member of our church, but I had never met him personally. Our church is a rather large church.

Over the next few days, Attorney Raheim prepared what was needed to request the judge to reconsider. We did not have to formally go to court for the request to be made. He asked the judge and she said, "No." And that was that. We decided to at least go back to court to get the "slave bracelet" removed. The judge also denied that request but stated that Dante could have a curfew that would give him until 11:00 p.m. to be indoors. Remember, his initial order was a 24-7 house arrest, except on the days that he would go on field trips and meetings with the youth group.

By the summer of 2015, the court sessions continued with one continuance after another. Attorney Raheim inquired of the judge to have the "slave bracelet" removed again. Eventually, she said, "yes." After the court session, the attorney immediately telephoned the Probation Officer to let him know that the judge okayed the request to remove the bracelet.

I traveled with Dante straight to the probation office. The officer cut the bracelet off with a pair of paper scissors as he had done a few months prior, and stated, hopefully it is for good this time. He was really a rather "cool" officer. He was not going to stick his neck out for Dante, however, even though he considered him to be a really good kid. He would often say his job is to do as he is told. He wrote the probationary reports as he saw fit. I never saw any of the reports that were submitted to the courts, but the officer stated that they were all good. He does his part and then the court does the rest, he would often say.

Chapter 22
The Public Service Officials

As Dante's case was now at a standstill, I decided to once again reach out to the public and elected officials. I initially reached out to our senator regarding the $500,000 "murder bond" that was given to Dante at the beginning of the case. I also felt the need to reach out again to him but to broaden my efforts of outreach. I should be able to get someone to help. I telephoned the State Representatives, the Congressman, a few senators and even the Governor. All calls were returned, and all the public officials were again empathetic to Dante's story. However, all public officials appeared to be stuck.

I wanted the officials to have the statute for the Diversion Program enforced. I informed them of this. All officials appeared to pass the buck. One official stated that it was the other officials' role to become more involved. All officials agreed on one issue, however, that the judicial system is a hard nut to crack and does need to change. That message was crystal clear. The game in that system is "wrapped up" tightly, they would say. Well, that is a big problem, I thought to myself. The checks and balances need to be enforced. The director of Dante's outpatient program stated during one of our treatment meetings, "What good is it to have laws and statutes on the books if we are not going to use or enforce them?"

The Public officials appeared to have a bipartisan attitude towards the issue of Mental Health. They all appeared to want to correct the flaws, but just appeared to be stuck on how to do so.

As I reflect on how empathetic the officials sounded during my conversations with them, it is hard for me to have negative feelings regarding them. I also realized that Dante's case was somewhat unique. If your own family is not directly impacted by someone with a mental health condition, it can be very difficult to understand the magnitude of the illness.

Even when the professionals study the issue of mental illness/mental health conditions, the assessments may be inaccurate if you are not totally immersed and in tune with the scope and study of such illnesses. It is up to those of us who are dealing with these issues directly to become as educated as possible regarding the broad scope of stages and types of mental illnesses. We must continue the conversation and raise awareness to reduce the stigma so that appropriate policies can be made and enforced.

One community leader, Mr. Wilson, did reach out to the Regional Mental Health Board in attempts to get to the bottom of the issue. He spoke with the Executive Director who explained the process to Mr. Wilson as he understood it. Mr. Wilson telephoned me back to help me see the bright side of things. If you go with the Mental Health defense, which was what we had now been discussing with Attorney Raheim, at least Dante would not get a criminal record.

"Lord knows we do not need any more young Black males with a criminal record in this country," he said.

I did agree with that.

Chapter 23
Back to Court Again

I am not sure if the change in the Judge was due to my conversation with one public official, but at the next court session, there was a new judge, Judge Brown. The word around town was that he could be more difficult than Judge White. He was an African American judge. Sometimes, that comes with its own stand-alone issues. Sometimes, judges of color feel that they have more to prove and may be harsher. Judge Brown did not make any concrete decisions as it related to Dante's case. Dante's case remained in a continuance mode until the end of the year when it was finally decided that the Mental Health defense would be used. This defense was only decided because there was a total lack of understanding of the case; the investigation was never thorough, and there seemed to be a civil war within the prosecution team on how the case should be handled.

There were some on the prosecution team who acknowledged in court and in writing that Dante had been progressing well and would not object to a diversion program for him. There were others, including the lead prosecutor, who felt that no matter what, Dante should go to jail, even though he had a mental health condition and had no prior criminal record. The prosecutor who felt that way appeared to buy into the stereotype that young Black males belong behind bars, just my opinion. He also may have just wanted to win a case. One never knows.

After our attorney decided that we would try the Mental Health defense, I did ask the attorney to inquire about the Diversion Program once again with the new Judge. The attorney then told me that he already had. Since the new judge had rejected the request, he did not want to further stress my life, so he did not mention it to me. I did ask the attorney why was the request rejected? Attorney Raheim stated that the new judge had a completely different reason from Judge White, once again, leading me to believe that there is obviously a lot of subjectivity in the decision-making process within the Judicial System.

And so it went....

Chapter 24
The Mental Health Defense

For whatever reason, Dante had to first prove that he had been diagnosed with a mental health disorder before the case could move forward. Dante had been diagnosed with Bi-Polar Disorder two years prior. He had one psychotic break, was hospitalized and released. He remained stable until his second psychotic break, two years later. His second psychotic break led to the need for this story to be told.

Our Attorney had him assessed again by yet another Psychiatrist. Dante had now had several assessments completed to prove that he had a formal diagnosis, not to mention that Big Dante had also been diagnosed with a similar disorder about fifteen years prior. Luckily, Big Dante never had a brush with the law that led to such stigmatization and confusion.

A change in Dante's diagnosis did occur after this second psychotic break. Once Dante began to receive treatment from his outpatient program, the Psychiatrist there studied Dante's symptoms and episode a little more in depth and gave him the diagnosis of Schizoaffective Disorder, Bi-polar1 type. This disorder is a mixture of schizophrenia and bipolar disorder. The follow-up Psychiatrist came to the same conclusion as did a third Psychiatrist who assessed Dante for the Mental Health Defense.

As Attorney Raheim had never fought a case using the Mental Health Defense, he had to do a lot of studying. As I began to question others regarding this defense, I learned that it is not a defense that is usually used to fight a case. The more our attorney studied this defense, the leerier he became. He wanted to change his mind, stating that he somewhat feared the defense. He stated that the defense and plea reminded him of the movie "One Flew Over the Cuckoo's Nest," the more that he researched and studied. I felt that society had progressed way beyond a 1975 movie and that it should be okay to pursue. Was I mistaken?

At this point, the lead prosecutor decided that he wanted Dante to go to jail and was not budging on any offers Attorney Raheim tried to negotiate. I did believe that the entire case eventually became personal, and Dante had been caught in the middle. The case was no longer about Dante. I felt that we had no choice but to use the Mental Health Defense.

I was a Social Worker; maybe not a licensed clinical social worker, but a Social Worker, nonetheless. I felt that if Dante were placed in an environment where the professionals understood mental health and mental health conditions, the outcome could only be positive. The attorney referred to the statute that he would be using to defend the case: CGS 584-17a. The statute seemed clear and direct to me. Dante had been stable and living at home, taking his medications; he had wrap-around therapy services, had obtained employment, and his license.

What could possibly go wrong? The assessors would be able to see that he is stable and refer him back to the outpatient program. **NOT.**

Chapter 25
The Trial

A very short court session was held, and the decision was made that the Mental Health Defense would be used. Shortly afterwards, the media printed another *Breaking News* story, "Mental Health Defense Planned for Teen."

The trial was scheduled on a very cold winter morning. Several family members came to court on this day to support Dante, including his Uncle Calvin who had been traveling back and forth from Pennsylvania to offer as much support as possible. Dante's clinical team from his outpatient program, along with the Forensic Psychiatrist, also came to testify and speak on Dante's behalf. I wanted to be called to the stand, but for whatever reason, Attorney Raheim did not think that it would be such a good idea. He was leery of the cross examination that I would receive. The attorney felt that I was too emotionally involved.

The trial did not last very long. The prosecutor only had one family member show up. She only showed up because she had been subpoenaed. Others were subpoenaed but did not show. As I am writing, I am thinking, "Isn't that against the law to just not show up?" My attorney thought that the entire family would be there, including the little girl that Dante had been accused of hitting with the car. There were approximately 40 family members that could have come. I had mixed feelings about their "no show." I was happy on one hand, but also curious on the other hand as to why they did not come. The police officer came out for the prosecution but testified as if he were speaking on behalf of Dante. He was the same officer who had called two years prior with the news that no one was hurt, but that Dante was in trouble. He appeared to be honest, but his testimony was a bit confusing.

Dante's clinical team from the outpatient program testified that he had been progressing well in the outpatient youth program. He was eligible to participate in their program until he was 26 years old, they informed the judge.

There was a lunch break, and the judge came back with his ruling.

"Not Guilty by Reason of Mental Disease."

Our family thought that the ruling was a good one but were all surprised when they took Dante away in handcuffs, anyway. The Psychiatrist was not surprised, nor was our attorney. I would only find out later that Dante was not that surprised because he had been forewarned by the Psychiatrist and our attorney that this action might happen, even with a "Not guilty" verdict.

I was again left out of the loop for supposed fear of my stress level. If I had known that they were going to take Dante away no matter what, I would not have insisted that he wear his Sunday red power tie and best Sunday shoes.

The attorney met with the family after they took Dante away, and explained that he would be housed at the Forensic Institute for approximately sixty days for an evaluation, and then we would all come back to court for the final ruling.

Again, even though disappointed, I felt Dante's mind was now stable; the professionals would recognize this and release him. There would be no reason to keep him.

Chapter 26
The Forensic Institute

Shortly after Dante arrived at the Forensic Institute, he was able to call. He sounded a bit shaken and said that he tried to explain to the many people there that were asking him questions about what had just transpired. He had arrived there in a suit and tie. A couple of staffers commented about his clothing, but not in a bad way, he said. They just alluded to the fact that it was not usual. I later learned that most others come there from another hospital setting or the Department of Corrections. Dante had come from home, where, incidentally, he had been doing well for almost two years.

The Forensic Institute can be a controversial place. After finally getting the approval to visit Dante, I went to visit. While in the waiting room, I read an article that had been placed in the information bins for the visitors to read. I would eventually come to read and take these articles home on every visit to see if there was something new that I could learn. There was one such article labeled the *Hospital Psychiatry Textbook*. The textbook summarizes the institute as such:

> The focus of the institute is to provide clinical treatment and care to those who have a treatable psychiatric condition. The misuse of the Forensic Institute for those who have not been diagnosed with a mental illness or who would not otherwise require hospital level care contributes to the stigma of mental illness. Valuable resources are wasted, it stated. Inappropriately placed individuals contribute to poor bed utilization and discharge planning.

I totally agreed with this summation. I felt that Dante was inappropriately placed, initially. Some are placed there to avoid going to jail. If there is no mental illness, I feel that this is wrong to place someone in such an institution. Some are placed there and appear to be held there too long. And some actually appear to be appropriately placed. The whole situation is not a one size fits all situation. The plans have to be individualized. Dante had been diagnosed with a psychiatric mental health condition but was stabilized prior to entering the Forensic Institute. If the courts felt the need to just place him somewhere, there are less restrictive settings where he could have been placed. It would probably still have been an inappropriate placement, but it would have been more fitting.

Either way, on the day Dante was transported to the Forensic Institute, the media felt that it was another *Breaking News* story, and wrote, "Teen Found Not Guilty by Reason of Mental Disease." This story was not bad. It was written with a more positive tone than some of the others that had previously been written. Attorney Raheim was spotlighted as successfully arguing the case.

I told Dante about the news article since he did not see it. Once in the Forensic Institute, access to the social media is gone. In my opinion, that is not necessarily a bad thing, for a while, anyway. The "patients" as they call them, are able to have complete television access, with all of the cable channels; the "not guilty " news was not reported on television like the initial reports of Dante's "crime" were. The reports where Dante was labeled a criminal, were more newsworthy, I concluded.

Dante was initially placed on a co-ed floor. I spoke with the Social Worker on this floor almost daily after I finally found her. Initially, it was very difficult to locate the staff of the institute. I called all over the place to connect with the right person, The Social Worker seemed nice enough after I found her. She explained that our family may be in over our heads with the Plea of Not Guilty by Reason of Insanity. This Plea is usually used for more severe cases, she stated. I tried to explain to the Social Worker why the family thought that we had no choice but to go this route. We discussed the CGS 17a-582. The Social Worker stated that the statute is written on the books, but the hospital does not really pay any attention to it. The Social Worker said, "good luck," and that would be the last conversation that I had with that particular Social Worker.

Dante was hit on the head within his first week of stay on the co-ed unit of the Forensic Institute. Dante said that he was not hit hard and knew he that the patient who hit him was mentally ill. He explained to the patient that it was not cool to hit, and the patient backed off, Dante said. I did complain. The next day, Dante was moved to another floor where the patients were supposed to be more stable, but they were also slated to remain in the facility longer term. When I called the unit to speak with Dante, a patient answered the phone. She told me that Dante had been moved to another floor. Without me asking why, she decided to offer the information that Dante had been moved to another floor because he would automatically be staying in the facility long term, she was told.

I did not think much about her comment at the time as she was a patient. In hindsight, her comment would prove to be instrumental. Dante was supposedly placed in the Forensic Institute for a 60-day evaluation.

I telephoned Dante on the new unit to get his take on why he had been moved. He said that the floor was supposed to be more stable. The rooms did appear a bit "more free," he stated. I spoke with the new Social Worker on the floor; he appeared nice enough. He stated that Dante would remain on the current unit until he went back to court. He sounded fair.

I telephoned Dante daily during his stay on this unit. He appeared to be adjusting to the unit and taking in his new surroundings. He did say that he would wake up on occasion and think that he was still at home. I tried to assure him that, after this "evaluation period," this should all be over. The evaluators appeared to have conflicting opinions on the direction that Dante's case should go. Again, in hindsight, those clinicians who worked on Dante's case and evaluated him solely on stability, appeared to be ready to release him. Those who knew that Dante was admitted with the

NGRI (Not Guilty by Reason of Insanity) plea seemed to feel that Dante should be kept in the Forensic Institute, no matter what. Even though the statute clearly states that all patients do not have to be confined, this is how it has been done historically and that is what we will keep doing, the opposing clinicians seemed to feel.

Chapter 27
Back to Court Again

Sixty days had come and gone. Dante was scheduled for pick up on his initial court date. There was a mix up in the transportation arrangements, and somehow Dante was never picked up for court. Court was rescheduled for a couple of weeks later. I called the governor on this afternoon. He returned the call and tried to pacify me. People do get out of there, he said.

A couple of weeks passed, and we would have the same judge presiding as we had 60 days prior. The court session was not as positive this go around. It was very short, as if it had been predetermined. Our attorney pled the case and did an excellent job, in my opinion. The cards had already been stacked. All his objections were overruled, and the judge made a rather quick decision after getting the reminder from the prosecution on what the decision should be.

To me, we could have skipped that court session. Minds had already been made up. Dante requested to speak on his own behalf. He did an excellent job. The judge was moved, but not enough. He obviously had a previous order to fill and could not be swayed by anything that was said. And so it went. Twenty-one years under the Psychiatric Review Board was ordered, the max that could be given for such crimes. Attorney Raheim could have objected again at this point, but my intuition says that he gave up and said, what's the use. It will be overruled.

Chapter 28
The Judge Had No Clue (The Verdict in Review)

"For a split second, I thought that the judge was going to actually do the right thing," Dante said after the final verdict.

"Twenty-one years," the judge said after leaning over to the prosecution team to inquire how much time he should say.

It was up to him to weigh the facts and evidence. He was supposed to decide, but appeared to have forgotten what decision he was supposed to make. It seemed like he did not take into consideration the previous evidence that was presented. It had all become a social game.

Even after that ridiculous verdict, Dante found something positive to say, a trait I suppose he inherited from me. My son had the audacity to say that 21 is actually his favorite number, so it must have some significance.

How the judge came to his verdict was unfortunate. He relied on the assessment of one Social Worker with the same degree that I have. Not minimizing Social Work degrees, but when you also have the assessment of a doctor with a degree in psychiatry, and the Social Worker's assessment takes precedence, it makes you question such a thought process.

To give a Social Worker so much power is harmful, especially when the assessment is incorrect. During the cross examination by our attorney, she admitted that she basically writes the same assessment for everyone who pleads "Not Guilty By Reason of Mental Disease." To make matters worse, she had done so for the last 10 years!

Even after such an admission, the judge gave this ruling. He did not appear to have much experience with mental health cases. This was evidenced by the fact that he asked the psychiatrist the meaning of P-S-Y-C-H-O-S-I-S, at least twice and how to spell it.

Had the Social Worker written an accurate assessment, the entire outcome of the case would have been different because this Superior Court Judge, appeared uninformed.

Chapter 29
The First Episode

At this moment, I feel the need to share a bit more history on how we ended up in such a mess with the mental health and judicial systems. It is important to go back to my son's first episode in order to do so.

I admittedly had ignored the forewarnings. I was not totally unaware of bipolar disorder, like Kerri Whitmore in the novel, *72 Hour Hold*. However, the sudden upsurge did come from out of nowhere as did her daughter's bi-polar disorder. In our case, I had been dealing with a husband, who had been diagnosed with bipolar disorder quite a few years prior.

I have no other way to describe it, except that it is an extremely annoying disease, if untreated. For most of the years with my husband, I dealt with a man who refused to acknowledge, let alone get treatment for bipolar disorder. I would eventually choose not to deal with it anymore and I got a divorce. In hindsight, was this the best way to handle his disorder? Maybe not.

My husband did not want to accept the diagnosis of bipolar disorder, and therefore rarely took the prescribed medication. In addition to this, in his younger years, he was a rather heavy drinker. This behavior led to constant turmoil and an inability for us to communicate. Not before too long, I just gave up.

Was it some type of karma that my son inherited this same disorder? I would like to think not. It was just the deck of cards that he was dealt. Inheriting bipolar was a part of it. My son was almost 17 when he was given the diagnosis of bipolar disorder. This is exactly the time that most are diagnosed, according to the researchers.

My son Dante's first psychotic break occurred in the late summer of 2012. He and my daughter had taken a bus trip to Pennsylvania to rehearse for my brother's wedding. I was scheduled to drive down later along with my husband who was also in the wedding, but of course, he did not need any practice because, as he said, "I am just that great."

I soon got a call after the kids arrived. I was in a training session for my new job working with the government. My daughter, my mom, and other family members were witnessing my son's first psychotic break and were in a panic trying to describe to me what was happening.

"Have you ever seen anything like this before?" my dad asked when he called.

"I actually have," I replied.

But not with Dante; with his dad, Big Dante, as we called him.

Big Dante was not big or tall. He was, about 5 feet 8 inches, handsome and brown-skinned, with light brown eyes. We just called him Big Dante because there had to be something to distinguish him from his son, since they shared the same name.

Dante had been working on a paper for school that would enable him to graduate on time. For whatever reason, he decided to write about the government and the controls that it supposedly had on genetically modified foods, GMO's. All of this research seemed to trigger a paranoia about the government.

As told to me by his sister, he spoke about the government controlling the U.S. population with chips that would be placed in the arm of every citizen's arm and could track their movements. He deleted his Facebook page for fear of being watched. The physical psychosis occurred when he ran into the streets of a town in Pennsylvania to warn the people of that town that they were in trouble and that the world was coming to an end. My daughter stated that, as he was doing this, he just kept tearing up stating that he did not know what was happening to him and felt something was wrong with him. He seemed scared of himself, she said.

Dante ran through the streets and onto the highway of the town. His 77-year-old grandad ran after him but could not catch him. His grandad decided to go back and get the car to try and catch up with him. His grandad did catch him as he was about to enter a truck to warn the driver that the world was coming to an end. He was able to stop him and put him in the car, but Dante got away again and ran to a construction site where he began to "preach" to the workers.

Dante's grandad remembers rather vividly that the sermon Dante preached was coherent and a good one. He was impressed by whatever was said. Dante's sister tried to explain to their grandad that Dante never talks in such a manner, and she had no clue where such a "sermon" would come from. The police were called as Dante was preaching. He was preaching uncontrollably and was unable to listen to voices of reason.

He began to curse once the police arrived. They took him away in their car, but not to jail, straight to the hospital. This Pennsylvania force obviously had training on mental health issues to know to take him to the hospital. They could have easily found something to take a Black man to jail for, which they usually do.

Dante stayed in the hospital for about a week in Pennsylvania before being transported back home by ambulance to Connecticut for follow up. The wedding went on as planned. One groomsman had the privilege of walking two ladies down the aisle. He took Dante's place. It was an outside tent wedding on a hill; the colors were maroon and gold. There appeared to be no further drama on that day, and the day proceeded according to plan.

Luckily, I was not in the wedding and was able to attend for a while. After the wedding, I went back to the hospital to sit with Dante who was still in a psychotic state. As this was his first episode, the whole family was in awe as to what to do or think. Big Dante's mania never seemed to manifest in such a way. Since big Dante was a drinker, maybe his episodes were masked? We would find out a couple of years later that Big Dante's and Dante's diagnoses were not exactly the same, and since the two diagnosis were not exactly the same, they may have manifested in different ways.

Once Dante returned to Connecticut, he was immediately taken to the St. Francis Hospital, where he was stabilized on *Depakote, Cogentin,* and *Thorazine*. Once stabilized, the Psychologist tried to purposely say things that would agitate an unstable person to assure that he was stable. The Psychologist came out of the room and stated that he could go home now. "His mind is stable, and I can't 'shake' him," he said. He prescribed 500 milligrams of *Depakote* and discharged Dante.

Dante had already missed about a week of school. It was potentially his senior year, providing all of the requirements were met. He was definitely on the cusp of not making it. Metropolitan Learning Center for International and Global Studies had been the school that both he and his older sister attended after attending the Montessori School for their elementary education, the only two schools for academic preparation that both children knew. The school was advanced in its curriculum.

Upon graduating, I would never argue that both children were not provided with a well-rounded education. Dante struggled with grades a little more than his older sister, but he also did not study as hard. Even though Dante's grades did not reflect it, I feel he retained the same amount of education information to move forward in life as did his older sister.

Dante was happy to be back amongst his high school peers and made it through his last year of school. He also attended an outpatient program for teens at the Institute of Living. The Institute of Living was a well-known clinic in the area that historically had been a place of psychological treatment for the Hollywood stars when they could no longer handle the pressures of fame and the Hollywood lifestyle.

Dante completed his senior year with no medication in his system.

After hearing so many complaints from Dante about the side effects of the medicine and witnessing his lethargic demeanor daily, it also began to bother me. I admittedly went into denial regarding the need for so much medication.

Dante graduated on time. Shortly afterward, he obtained a full-time job with Wal Mart and was also accepted into the nearby Manchester Community College. He started with a couple of classes which he seemed to enjoy, but eventually started to get behind. He soon became overwhelmed and decided to just work instead.

Dante considered himself a hip-hop artist since he performed for the talent shows in high school and a couple of community shows. He enjoyed performing and it came easy for him. During his senior year, he was voted "Most Likely To Win a Grammy" by the senior class. With this thought in mind, Dante always felt that the jobs that he obtained were just side jobs that would help to advance his hip-hop career.

In Dante's effort to make more money, he obtained a second job, a third shift warehouse position with Home Goods Distribution Center. One would have never imagined, without awareness, the effects of this one position and how it would spiral into a second psychotic episode.

As Dante tried to hang onto this position, mostly for the extra money that he was making, he gradually became more manic due to the frustration of the position. The change in sleep pattern due to working third shift was also taking a toll on him, but none of us saw this at the time.

This history of events was the *segue* that led to Dante eventually having a second psychotic episode, go through the sequence of events just described in previous chapters that eventually landed him in the Forensic Institute.

Chapter 30
Back to the Forensic Institute

To the total shock of everyone, Dante was taken in handcuffs back to the Forensic Institute. I telephoned Dante later that evening. He was disappointed, but not totally shocked. The Forensic Social Worker had forewarned him that he would be returning to the Forensic Institute. The Social Worker had written that she and the team felt that Dante was a danger to society. The Social Worker also informed Dante that he should tell his attorney to fight to have him not placed under the Psychiatric Review Board. Attorney Raheim did attempt to do this, but since the same Social Worker who advised Dante to fight against placement under the board, wrote in her report that Dante is a danger to society, totally contradicting herself, Dante was placed under the Psychiatric Review Board.

The judge forgot about the previous court case where many spoke highly of Dante, and made his final decision based on a report that was devised after sixty days of a semi-observation. The outpatient clinical team that had been working with Dante for over a year and a half was no longer of any use to the judge. Their report was too positive. A report stating that Dante was a danger to society is what was needed to place Dante back into the Forensic Institute.

I am not sure if the Social Worker agreed with the report that she presented to the court, but it became clear that Dante may have been needed to fill a Forensic Hospital bed. He had been stabilized for almost two years. He was not a problem on the units of the Forensic Institute. He deescalated potentially dangerous situations on the unit when staff were not around. His demeanor was not even dangerous when he had his psychotic break. The situation could have been more serious. The victims were not that afraid of Dante or they would not have assaulted him. Dante says if the police had not shown up, he could have died. The elderly lady had obviously not been that afraid either if she went back to the car to grab Dante. I don't want to minimize all that happened on the day in question, but the punishment has been overkill, especially since Dante was the only one left with cuts and bruises.

The media did capture Dante with the bruises. All his pictures that were displayed on the news and in the newspapers had pictures with the bruises and a chipped tooth. The media also decided to print another article after the second portion of the trial:

> "Teen committed to the Forensic Institute; Judge calls him a Danger."

The reporter wrote the lead story, and the local newspapers followed suit. The stories varied from one newspaper to another, as usual. I did telephone the reporter to inform him that I did not appreciate the article. He insisted that he had written the story as it happened. The reporter had spoken with Dante on a few occasions throughout the court case. He would often tell me what a respectable young man he seemed to be. Even with that said, this same reporter had no problem writing an article stating that Dante was a danger.

Chapter 31
"The Jail for White Privilege? "

Dante was able to write about and verbalize the events of the day his psychotic break occurred once he became stabilized and placed in the Forensic Institute. I have come to affectionately call the institute "the jail for whites." Many of the people who have been placed there have committed very serious and violent crimes. People have murdered their parents, one even with an axe. Coincidentally, many of the more violent crimes were committed by whites. In order to be placed within the Forensic Institute, you are supposed to have a diagnosis of mental illness. I will add that my son has now interacted with some of the aforementioned people. He defended them and opposes some of my thinking when I discuss the seriousness of their crimes compared to what occurred on his unfortunate day of events. He has now conversed with them, and declares that, in their "right" minds, these people are some of the nicest people you could ever meet. I am admittedly struggling with all of this. Many emotions and notions regarding the whole concept of the Forensic Institute continue to plague me. I will restate again, writing about this has been cathartic.

I understand that my son committed a "crime," but no one was hurt, (except for him). He does have a diagnosis of Schizoaffective Disorder, but somehow, he was easily placed amongst people who had committed much more serious and violent crimes.

My son was given a job in the library while placed in the institute and began to read more and more. They wanted to keep him mentally occupied. He had always been fond of reading, as long as he was reading something that was of interest to him. In his renewed found love of reading, he began to read more challenging topics. He stumbled upon Dr. Martin Luther King's "Letter from Birmingham Jail." He decided to devise his own letter entitled "Letter from the Forensic Institute." He included the recollection of events from the day that changed all our lives forever. He also included in that letter why he felt that he should not be institutionalized. I have also included these reasons in a subsequent chapter.

Chapter 32
Money, Power, Greed

It became apparent that many egos and money had driven this case. Somewhere along the line, all involved forgot that the case was about Dante. Money appeared to drive the entire system. The bail bondsman was even still in the picture. He said that he needed more money. The initial bail was $500,000. This amount was not paid off, he said. There had now been three lawyers on the case. And yet still another lawyer was needed to deal with the bail bondsman. Attorney Raheim referred the family to Attorney Kente to work with the bondsman as he was unable to handle both situations at the same time. A conflict of interest or something, he said. I kept thinking about how our financially struggling family helped to keep so many people employed throughout the case.

If everyone had only told the truth from the very beginning, the case could have been resolved in six months. Dante would have gone to the hospital from the beginning, like he should have. He would have been stabilized and released, maybe. I can't forget he is Black, and just because of this, there is a stronger feeling that he must pay. If he was not going to go to jail for what had occurred, he must be confined somewhere. I tend to forget that this appeared to be the school of thought. There is more money to be made by confining him to the Forensic Institute. That is the only explanation I could think of for such behavior by professionals. I would love to also think that the system is just that flawed, that no one talks to each other, but money is still the underlying factor I am sure.

Chapter 33
The Psychiatric Review Board

Dante embraced his stay at the Forensic Institute over the next few months. He participated in all the Institute had to offer. To my surprise, it had more to offer than I thought. If the criminal element is taken out of the equation, it could be a rather positive place. Many groups were offered that Dante took advantage of: a men's group, a coffee group, a hanging on the corner group, an insanity plea group, an art club, a fitness group, a mental health group, yoga. There was an upper gym, a lower gym, a weight room with machine weights. There were outdoor baseball and basketball games, not to mention volleyball and board games. There is bingo where you can win prizes, like UConn paraphernalia. They have a Play Station room and another room for watching movies and a few rooms to watch television. If the cards are played right, it does not appear to be a bad deal. You are confined away from the rest of the world, however, but even this could be embraced, depending on the type of person that you are.

Dante had been working on a hip-hop career before entering the institute. There was a Musical Art Teacher at the institute who took an interest in Dante's story regarding his goal of becoming a hip-hop artist. The art teacher produced a talent show for the patients and staff of the institute. Dante was the " headliner." He wrote a hip-hop song specifically for the talent show. He was somewhat excited about performing the song, even if his family was unable to see his performance. He thought of the performance as practice for when he can perform again for an audience. I must state that he had just performed for the Board of Directors for the outpatient program just a few days prior to entering the Forensic Institute. He was not considered a danger there.

Dante performed for the patients and staff of the Forensic Institute a couple of days prior to his first scheduled meeting with the

Psychiatric Review Board. I met with Dante's clinical team prior to the Review Board meeting. The team stated that Dante continues to do well. I thought that we were all on the same page after the conclusion of the meeting. The team was supposed to present a plan to the Psychiatric Review Board to move Dante to a less restrictive setting.

On the day of Dante's hearing in front of the Review Board, the Forensic police brought Dante to the Review Board meeting in handcuffs. This is standard procedure, I was told. So even if he was found Not Guilty by Reason of Mental Disease, he is still considered a criminal as evidenced by the handcuffs. The sight of a black male man in handcuffs removes any doubt that he is 'a criminal' and must be kept locked up. The Review Board meeting was awful, extremely disappointing, as the team was not able to speak as a group. The lead Psychiatrist was able to speak, but she was overpowered by the Forensic Social Worker, the same one who had initially told Dante to fight to not go under the board but wrote in her assessment that he needed to do so.

I excused myself from the room. I could no longer take the lies and needed to compose myself before I did something that I might regret. The unit Social Worker came out to see if I was okay. She said she knows that the system "sucks," but they will continue to work to get Dante moved. She seemed sincere with her comments, but unfortunately, the final decision was not up to her. There appeared to be an establishment working that had been in existence for many years. The establishment must have money attached to it, was all I continued to think. The Review Board decided that Dante would remain in the Forensic Institute because he was still a danger, according to the report given by the Forensic Social Worker.

After the hearing, I was finally able to briefly speak to the Forensic Social Worker who had produced and reported the incorrect assessment. She had completely ignored me up until this point. I let her know that her report was inaccurate, and I reminded her that I think that she already knew that. She kept walking and stated that she will no longer be on the case. I told her "good," and walked away as well.

The Psychiatric Board would play a role throughout the remainder of Dante's case. After about a year, they did approve the decision to move Dante to a less restrictive setting. An application had initially been filed by the Forensic Institute to do so. The Board Director did state that they take their cues from the Forensic Institute. The Forensic Institute staff say that they take their cues from the board. There is an obvious catch-22 cyclical system going on there, I said to myself.

Dante wrote a nice essay not too long after his transition to the lesser restrictive setting. He entitled the essay:

"I Could Be Wrong, But What About My Rights?"

I am going to conclude this chapter with an excerpt from that essay regarding the Psychiatric Review Board.

In Dante's Words:

"I would like to speak on where they went right as it relates to the Psychiatric Review Board. Although I have skepticism and flat out disagree on how the board operates on most occasions. I will say that knowing that a person's mental health functioning is such a complex entity to decipher, I do believe the boards very extensive and very strict oversight over an acquittee may be necessary but only for a minority of extreme NGRI cases. The Psychiatric Review Board is separate entity from the Forensic Institute but appears to have the power to overrule the decision makers of the Forensic Institute when they feel that they need to. I do feel that power can be a nuisance but, on many levels, can be helpful. I say this only because before the board was created, I was told by other patients that the hospital mistakenly discharged a couple of acquitted patients based on the hospital opinion. They ultimately and unfortunately had to return to confinement for reasons I would rather not mention in this essay.

I do believe that these cases are now few and far in between as the facts show that it is much more rare for an NGRI acquittee to commit a criminal offense once released from the hospital, than someone that is released from the Department of Corrections. I write all this to say that I do get the point that there may be a need for a board and actually believe for more high risk NGRI acquittees the boards oversight and insight may prove to be a positive benefit in ensuring community safety."

Dante goes on to write in his essay conclusion:

"Regarding me, however, I will conclude by saying my confinement, whether it be maximum or minimum, is no longer warranted. I have shown that I can be a positive member of society without being a danger to myself or others. While out on bond for almost two years, I fought my case within the court system and maintained mental stability. I participated in an outpatient treatment program for young adults and was consistent with this treatment. I met weekly with my employment specialist, my psychotherapist, case manager and monthly with my psychiatrist. My time with this outpatient treatment program was beneficial for my mental health. I learned to identify triggers and talk out psychological social issues with my therapist. I worked on my resume and pursued job opportunities with my employment specialist. I actually was hired to work for Starbucks just prior to entering the Forensic Institute. I worked on organizing issues with my case manager and relayed medication issues to my psychiatrist. During this same two years, I also had to participate in a pre-trial probation where I had weekly check-ins with a probation officer and gave drugs tests that were clean every time because I was not a drug or alcohol user. I had a good rapport with the probation officer as well. I also had to follow a temporary curfew that was implemented by the court system.

In summary, I am someone with a clean history when it comes to behavioral or drug use and currently there are no indicators that I would be a threat to the community now or in the future if I maintain taking my current therapeutic dosage of medication, seek treatment in outpatient care and continue the course that I have been on for a few years now."

End of Dante's thoughts on the subject.

My thoughts:

I would like to add that if the Psychiatric Review Board really got to know the patients by interacting with them on some level, I may agree with their benefit. Currently the board appears to get second hand information that may not always be true and accurate. The fact that the board is making very concrete decisions about a patient's future livelihood is/was concerning to me. I feel that all board members should have extensive training on mental health conditions. It is my understanding that the board was comprised of various disciplines. If one does not have a unique understanding of mental illness/mental health conditions, it can be difficult to make a sound, well rounded decision regarding the prognosis and the trajectory of a person/ "patient"diagnosed with a mental health condition. I would also like to add that if I were a trained Psychiatrist, Psychologist or someone that is responsible for making sound decisions as it relates to a patient's mental health, I would be offended by a board that is not made up of professionals in the Psychiatric profession overruling my decision making.

I will end with that as it appears that there has already been a lot of controversy over the actual need for a board.

Chapter 34
NAMI

As Dante continued to adjust to his new surroundings, I decided to become more involved with advocacy groups that support individuals with mental illness, and their families. The National Alliance on Mental Illness (NAMI), is a national grassroots organization that has been around for years. It has increased in its outreach efforts and continues to grow with each passing year. My involvement with this organization has been completely positive. The information that is offered via this organization is the most up to date information one could ever find. The organization is the most progressive with reducing stigma that is associated with mental illness. They are instrumental in increasing education and awareness for those affected by mental illness directly, or who have a family member that is affected. They offer rather in-depth courses to help assist family members in coping with mental illness. The environment is welcoming, and since the environment is not intimidating, all who participate share stories and coping mechanisms for dealing with their situation. The most effective take away, I felt, is that you strongly get the sense that you are not alone in your struggle or situation.

One in every four persons is affected by mental illness, they would remind us. Newer studies have shown that the ratio may be even higher than that. The more conversation we have about mental illnesses, the more awareness will be raised and the less stigmatized it will become. That we must have the conversation is a constant theme of the organization.

I would later become a presenter for the NAMI "End the Silence" program for youth, work part-time for the organization, and become a member of their Board of Directors. I shared with Dante that I had become involved with this organization. He seemed to be elated by this news. He had been actively participating in therapy groups on his unit, and found them quite interesting, he would say.

Chapter 35
Dante Remains in The Forensic Institute

Dante remained in the Forensic Institute for a year after his initial hearing with the Psychiatric Review Board. It took that long for him to be moved to a lesser restrictive setting. He continued to embrace all that he could embrace while there. He continued work outs. He did lose weight and gain muscle. He ate okay meals and never complained about the food. The Institute would order take out dinner twice a month. Dante was designated to take the orders for all the guys on the floor. Many of the staff did recognize Dante's abilities to be responsible and would give him little assignments where he could exercise his skill. Dante's esteem was not low when he entered the Institute, but it increased even more as he learned all that he was capable of doing. He became a stronger baseball player and basketball player. He learned to play chess from some of the guys on the floor. He spent time in the library studying mental illness, amongst other things. I continued to talk to Dante daily and visit him weekly. I met with the team monthly, and they continued to report that they were working on a plan to get Dante out of there.

As they continued to tell me this over and over, I began to realize that, as much as they sincerely wanted to move Dante out, they were going to need help. I reached out to a legal team that advocates for persons with mental illnesses. I also had to hire Attorney # 5, Attorney Green. Attorney Raheim tried to do more, but I felt that he had run his course with a case involving a mental health condition as this was not his expertise.

Attorney Green had won a similar case a few years prior for a young man that had been placed under the Psychiatric Review Board. This attorney's information was given to Dante by a staff member who did not understand why Dante was still confined at the Institute. Dante telephoned me and provided me with the information so that I could reach out to the attorney.

I telephoned the attorney. I summarized the case the best I could without telling a forty-thousand-word story. The attorney stated that he had not worked a case quite like his previous mental health case in a long time case but would be willing to take the case on.

Coincidentally, not too long after the family retained attorney Green, another youth, who happened to be on Dante's floor, died in the Forensic Institute. Dante had also befriended this youth and stated that the youth looked up to him and had been asking Dante if he could come work out with him. Dante told him that he had to take his meds, because the youth did not like to take his meds. The youth had been having difficulty with the staff. Dante said that that he had been planning to work out with the youth before he died. The death of this youth bothered Dante tremendously, and the night he called to inform me that this situation occurred was the only time throughout Dante's stay at the Forensic Institute that I heard fear and hopelessness in his voice.

In the weeks following this occurrence, the patients on the unit did receive an extensive amount of group counseling around the patient's death. Dante eventually became lighthearted again, but this occurrence did greatly affect him.

Attorney Green heard about the incident and seemingly wanted to take on this case as well. The relationship with Attorney Green became strained very quickly. He had an interest in politics and appeared to have political motivations that made it difficult for him to devote the time needed to provide appropriate attention to Dante's case.

During one of my meetings with the senator a referral for yet another attorney was given. This group of attorneys worked directly with the judicial system and did have more understanding of the ins and outs, and red tape that is associated with the Insanity Defense and politics of the system in general. This group of attorneys did work and remain on the case. They were instrumental in having Dante moved to a less restrictive setting.

Chapter 36
The Burden of The Forensic Institute

As I continued to research and study the road that should be taken for those diagnosed with a mental illness/ mental health disorder, I continued to read articles while visiting the Forensic Institute. I did mention briefly a paragraph regarding the Burden of the Forensic Institute in an earlier chapter but felt the need to restate the point of this article in more depth. I feel that this article could also play a role in tackling overall prison reform.

There was a section of the article that indicated Forensic Institutes have a special burden, a dual mandate, was the term. They are supposed to provide clinical care to individuals while protecting the public. In order to do so, good treatment needs to be provided. This can occur when individuals are appropriately admitted for treatable psychiatric conditions that are the source of the risk to the community, it stated. It also stated that clinical administrators of Forensic units need to guard against the admission of individuals who pose a risk by virtue of criminality and antisocial personality because there is no credible end point for hospitalization of such individuals. The admission of some such individuals is often politically and legally unavoidable, but their presence is debilitating to the therapeutic milieu and staff morale, the article stated.

The article goes on to say that the misuse of forensic units for preventive detention of dangerous individuals who would otherwise not require hospital level care contributes to the stigma of mental illness and wastes resources that could be utilized for people with a serious mental illness that need enhanced security and have the potential to be rehabilitated. Inappropriately placed individuals contribute to poor bed utilization and patient flow to aftercare placements. Confining and containing offenders as punishment, or simply to prevent further offending may be legitimate for a criminal justice system, but should have no place in health service, the article then states, and I wholeheartedly agree.

Clinicians must be careful and focus their concerns on the clinical care of their patients and avoid the all too easy lapse of becoming agents of social control (Paul Mullen 2000).

I continued to think about these statements often while Dante was confined in the Institute. For the most part, for purposes of mental health treatment, Dante was almost appropriately placed if he just had to be placed somewhere to make the systems at play feel better. Dante's placement was strictly the combined decision of the court and the Forensic Institute.

From what we were told, the elderly victims involved stated that they wanted to see Dante get the help that he needed. The denial of the Diversion Program and the request for jail time all came from the prosecution team. From them and them alone, and even still, not all the prosecution team were in agreement with what should occur.

Chapter 37
Stress Relief Date

After all of the drama and stress of the recent months, a long-time male friend wanted to go out and have some fun. What do I have to lose, I thought to myself on this Friday evening? I had become overly exhausted by completely everything. I had engaged in fun activities here and there, but the movie of President Obama's first date with First Lady Michelle came out on this day. I had been waiting to see it. I liked Tika Sumpter who played the First Lady, and President Obama was just the man, and symbolic of a perfect gentleman, to me, so it did not matter who played him. The movie did not receive rave reviews, but I enjoyed it just the same, as I knew that I would.

I admired them as the First Couple and to see how they got together was of interest to me, even if the movie was corny. It was a short movie. Shorter than most. The night was still young after the movie was over. My friend, Lance, decided that he was hungry and that we should get something to eat. It was a little late for a heavy meal, but I went along and ate a salad with grilled chicken and just one roll. That was difficult to do as I am a bread addict. I'll choose bread over chocolate if I must choose between the two. There was a dance floor at the restaurant. He wanted to dance. As I was there to relieve stress on this evening, why not, I thought to myself. We danced for a while but soon left. He took me home. He was respectful, that night. The night ended and did prove to be a stress buster.

Chapter 38
The Legal Rights Project

The Legal Rights Project was a team of advocates that were housed on the Hospital's campus. I was informed by my friend, Sheila, to reach out to them as they may be able to help. I went straight to their offices to see what services they could provide. I coincidentally bumped into the Assistant Director and I proceeded to tell him the story of all that had occurred. He shook his head, but not with disbelief, more with the attitude of "here we go again." The sentiment of the ill treatment throughout the campus appeared to be universal, but so entrenched that no one knew how to correct the wrongs. The Assistant Director decided to complete the intake information for Dante and assign a personal advocate to his case.

Dante's advocate was good. She was strong willed and a real fighter who was determined to do the right thing. She knew that corruption had been pervasive throughout the campus and she was going to do whatever little or great amount she could do to make the rules work for Dante. She read Dante's record first, and eventually she told me, that after reading the record, she was a little afraid to meet Dante because the reports painted him as a monster! After meeting him, she was shocked to find such a gentleman, she said. More corruption, I thought silently to myself.

As the months moved forward, the advocate would consistently remind the treatment team that Dante was being held in a setting where he should not be. Eventually, the team agreed and filed an application to move Dante to a less restrictive setting. Shortly after Dante's application was submitted and approved, his advocate was laid-off. Always the good ones, I said again to myself.

Chapter 39
A Less Restrictive Setting

Dante was finally moved to a less restrictive setting in the summer of that year, 2017. The setting was entitled The Community Reentry program. This placement allows him to walk the grounds of the campus and go on day trips to various parks around the state with other patients in the group. The family was beginning to believe that Dante would finally be discharged from this corrupt institution.

Guys that were placed in the less restrictive setting were supposed to be less of a danger and preparing to return to community living. However, there did not seem to be a clear discharge plan for any of these individuals. As the guys on the unit got to know me, they would share some of their stories with me.

The "patients" had many forms of therapy groups and a level system that would indicate your level of freedom. Level One was the most restrictive and a Level Four would allow one to roam about the campus and go on day trips. Dante maintained a Level Four for the duration of his time within this setting. As with the more restrictive setting, he took advantage of all that was offered.

Some of the groups were mandated and others Dante participated in because the name of the group sounded interesting, like Cooking Therapy. Dante would call home to talk about some of the dishes that were prepared in that group. There was also the Meditation Group, the Art Group, the Music Group, the Intimacy Group, (don't ask), bingo, chess, basketball, volleyball, baseball, a bowling league and a host of other activities. No matter how many activities were offered, however, there was still the constant reminder that you are not free.

Dante did work while in this setting a few hours a week until the funding was temporarily cut. It was all related to an ongoing investigation of the facility, we were told. Eventually, the funding returned, and Dante was given a job working in horticulture. He seemed to enjoy learning this new skill. He initially worked in the dining room but stated that he liked horticulture better.

Dante maintained a positive attitude while in both settings at the Forensic Institute. It was obvious to the family, and eventually to staff, that he strived to be the best that he could be. He maintained a healthy weight and became very conscious of what went into his body. He did begin to become frustrated that the process to move up and out was taking so long. I had been even more frustrated, I feel. A placement that I thought would take 60 days was now going on three years!

While in this setting, Dante became more of an avid reader; he continued to write his hip-hop music. Along with this, he would write essays regarding 'going ons' of the Institute.

Chapter 40
Advocacy Unlimited

As the process to discharge to the community did not occur as quickly as we thought that it would, I once again had to muster strength to reach out for more advocacy support. I was randomly sent an email one night.

"Come voice your concerns regarding abuse allegations at the Forensic Institute."

Ok, I thought, I will be there.

A week or so later, I attended this meeting. The connection to this group of people was instant, just as it had been with NAMI. This group was fiery, and they were ready to tackle the system of abusers of the mentally ill. They filled the large meeting area with large sheets of easel paper, writing down ways to eradicate systems of abuse. They set days and times for action steps and follow up focus groups. I eventually told a synopsis of Dante's story. The advocates were ready to go and fight, even if it had to be done in disguise. I spoke with the Assistant Director of the program who would eventually go on to visit Dante regularly and become a consistent source of support.

I knew that the connection with this group would remain a part of our lives, just as NAMI would. I did eventually find out the two advocacy groups were somewhat at odds with regards to ideology. I decided that I needed both of them equally and believe their overall mission, goals and end game are the same. The politics would work itself out.

I began to get emails from both NAMI and Advocacy Unlimited about the same issues.

"Come out to the Legislative Office Building (LOB). Have your voice heard!"

I decided to do that too.

The media began to report on the abuse that had been occurring on the Forensic Institute/Hospital campus. As Dante's process seemed to be dragging along, even though he had been moved to a lesser restrictive setting, I decided now was definitely the time to up the ante and speak up and out regarding the systemic abuse and corruption that was occurring so pervasively throughout the campus.

My efforts paid off slowly, slowly. I was elated when a member of the advocacy group nominated me for an advocacy award that I was presented with at the annual dinner for the Regional Mental Health Board. Maya, who nominated me, could never begin to understand how much I needed that boost of energy at that time and how thankful I was for it. I would not feel completely deserving of the award, however, until Dante was freed, and systems have changed. The award was given in the name of Whitney and Edna Jacobs a couple who fought their entire lives to make things better for the mentally ill in the state. Both of their children had been diagnosed with schizophrenia.

Chapter 41
The Senator

One Republican Senator became very outspoken about "The Culture of Cruelty" as she termed it. She decided to call a public hearing and I decided to attend this hearing and testify. This Senator would go on to be instrumental in making things happen for Dante as she was very passionate about getting down to correcting the source of corruption.

I met with the Senator a couple of months after the hearing. She spent a great deal of time listening to the story and thinking of ways to help correct the wrongs that had occurred. She telephoned the NBC Special Investigative Reporter. He immediately left his office to come over and hear Dante's story. The Senator even told him to bring pizza because we would be there for a while. The reporter came right over, but he forgot the pizza.

He sat with me for the same length of time as the Senator and tried to make sense of Dante's story. The story that I am writing now is the story that I told the reporter.

As the reporter would scratch his head in disbelief regarding parts of the story, there were times when I just wanted to say, "welcome to being a young a Black Man in America." I held my tongue instead and decided to just write about it.

The reporter decided not to do an article on Dante at the moment. The web may have been too tangled for him and he wanted to hold off. The Senator continued to remain interested in Dante's case and attended his release hearing to get a better picture of what was going on specifically with his case as well as others that had been brought to her attention.

As Dante's stay in the lesser restrictive setting seemed to be moving even slower than the more restrictive setting, our family along with the new set of attorneys, filed an application for Dante's release. Dante's initial request for release was denied. There was no concrete justification for the denial. It was seemingly denied because the powers that be felt that they could, and so they did.

After the hearing, the Senator remained seemingly compassionate about rectifying any wrong doings that may have occurred. She telephoned and inquired of me to keep her informed of follow up proceedings that may occur.

The Senator had many questions regarding the reasons for denial and there was a brief "Tweet" written about the hearing by another new reporter who had been following all of the goings on of the "hospital" and the Senator herself.

The Senator did become instrumental in a subsequent hearing. I feel that her presence did help *segue* into allowing the approval of Dante to temporarily leave the facility eventually. The Senator did maintain a connection with our family until Dante's discharge.

Chapter 42

Corruption and the Abuse Investigation

As The Forensic Institute began to receive media attention for alleged abuse allegations, a second reporter that I met with was intrigued by Dante's story. He had been the lead reporter and investigator into the situation from The Courant. The abuse of a now elderly man by the staff had taken precedence. As Dante had not been abused by staffers (Thank God), the reporter wanted to continue his reporting on this investigation and keep a side eye watch with regards to Dante's case. Like the Senator, he asked to receive periodic updates on Dante's case.

The culture of cruelty was pervasive throughout the entire campus. The abusive culture had been going on for so long that many staffers did not appear to know right from wrong. Staffers reportedly abused again after the initial media reports were circulated. Many staff were terminated and arrested. A few were allowed to resign. One was able to still receive a $7,000 monthly pension after resigning. This became a separate investigation and is ongoing as of this writing. As the investigation is currently ongoing, I will proceed with telling our story. I do think that it is important to mention that the culture of The Institute was now being watched closely.

Chapter 43
The Karuna Conference

Dante was invited by the advocacy group to sit on a panel and speak at a conference about his journey and his time spent at The Forensic Institute. This was a special day. After twisting and turning the Community Reentry Program's arm, Dante was allowed to go. He was only allowed to go for a portion of the conference, but the experience proved to be a learning one all the same. Dante was able to personally meet with the reporter who had expressed an interest in his case; he was also on the panel.

Dante discovered on that day that he had public speaking skills that he was not aware of. He spoke of his journey and his experience while in the Forensic Institute. He was able to give a balanced report and recollection of events. He spoke of both the positives and negatives that he had experienced and observed. He commended the Community Reentry Program for allowing him the opportunity to come and speak. Even though he was unable to attend the entire conference, the director could have said no altogether. This would have been cruel, but this had been the culture of the campus, so it would not have been unheard of.

Dante got to meet others at the conference that had similar experiences, even though none quite as unique as his. He was able to participate in one mental health workshop and then had to be transported back to his program.

He thanked the director of the Advocacy Program for the opportunity to participate. The director offered Dante a part-time job to work with the agency. Unfortunately, due to the restrictions Dante had been placed under from the Psychiatric Review Board, he would be unable to take the job at that moment.

Chapter 44
The Emotional Distress

I was thankful for the positive moments such as Dante's participation in the Karuna Conference, but I did continue to feel off centered as we were still going through. I did have dreams and even nightmares regarding Dante's entire situation. The nightmares were not so bad that they haunted me, but they did occur and would wake me up out of my sleep. I would often write at these times and try to strategize to calm my nerves and to put things back into perspective.

My dreams would usually be about feeling stuck or trapped. I vividly remember dreaming about being stuck in a weird village with only dirt roads and teepee-like huts and no way of getting home or out of that community. That dream stayed with me for a while and I did look up the dream interpretation. The dream was interpreted to mean that changes need to take place in my life in order for me to move forward or that I had been working too hard and needed to take a break. Either of those interpretations could have been correct as I did feel stuck in many ways.

As mentioned in previous chapters I would take time for self by enjoying the company of a friend or friends and self-reflecting in a park. I had also become more active in church. I had loved gospel music since I was a little girl. To join the church choir seemed only fitting. There was a small conflict there too; however, nothing negative, but the singing voices of the choir were so beautiful to me that I would often just want to listen to the others around me singing instead of singing myself. The connection to the church and choir definitely kept my spirits motivated.

I do hate that despite my spiritual connections, I felt like I was fighting the battle of broken and corrupt systems alone. I know that many were empathetic to what had occurred within our family, but few knew how to give support or how to help fix it.

Only God was constant, I had to continue to say to self.

Dante remaining mentally stable and strong was also a tremendous positive throughout the entire journey. A negative mindset from him may have taken me over the edge in the opposite direction.

Chapter 45
Race and Racism

There are a different set of rules in society for Black folks, period. I think about racism and the state of Black America daily, a few times a day in fact. The older I have become and the more life experiences that I have, the more I began to think about race and how it may have entered into a particular situation.

The more we experience others, the more open minded we should become. One would think that the trajectory of thought would go in the opposite direction. My personal experiences in life have led me to believe that the world is even more racially biased than I could have ever imagined.

Dante's case ran its course right along with the hoopla of racially charged politics going on in the country. The case ran through the end of the Obama administration and the beginning of the Trump administration, a.k.a the historic transition of a lifetime, (It will be known as that eventually). Knowing that the path of Dante's case had more to do with the color of skin than anything else, just added more fury to this fire for me.

The most frustrating part is that no one seems to know how to make the illness of racism and racial bias better. Both sides seem to really think that they are right in their thought processes. That is also why I often use the word racially biased as opposed to racist because those are "softer" words, and many who we may think and say are racist seem to sincerely think that they are not. So, in an effort to confront racists who don't think that they are, I have decided to address them as racially biased so that they can understand and hopefully alleviate defensive barriers. The word racist just seems to garner an automatic defensive reaction.

The Movie *Marshall*[2]

I had a number of "stress relief dates" during the stretch of advocating for Dante. On one evening in particular, I went with Big Dante to see the movie *Marshall*. Big Dante became more of a support mechanism for dealing with the whole ordeal. The movie *Marshall* was playing at select theaters and I really wanted to see it on opening night. Surprisingly, and now in hindsight, not so surprisingly, the movie was not playing at our local theater, the theater where many blacks frequent. The theater would have brought in a good revenue for the weekend. I continue to wonder why the movie was not offered at this particular theater. Did the owners feel that it would stir up controversy? The movie was set in Bridgeport, Connecticut in the 1940's. It revealed the deep racist attitudes of many Connecticut citizens during that time.

I thought about the *Marshall* movie for weeks after seeing it. I thought about how the case was tried in a Connecticut court by a racist judicial system that would not allow Thurgood Marshall ([1*]) to argue his case in court because Black lawyers were not allowed a license in the State of Connecticut. There was a scene in the movie where an acquaintance of Marshall's was also a Black lawyer by trade. He lived in Connecticut and had graduated from Fordham Law School. He stated that, even though he passed the bar, the State of Connecticut would not allow him to get a license to practice law but did allow him to get a driver's license, so he decided to become a driver to put food on the table and provide for his family. I also thought about how that entire situation did not occur generations ago, but only one generation ago. Those

---

[2] *(*) Thurgood Marshall was appointed by President Lyndon B. Johnson to the Supreme Court Justice on 10/1/1967. He was the first African American to receive this lifetime appointment. He served on the supreme court until the age of 81 years old and died a few years later at the age of 84 years old.*

who were born in that year would now be in their late seventies. Their children would be about my age give or take a few years. The attitudes of the protesters and the judges and the prosecutor were pretty bad during that year. I am now supposed to believe that those attitudes are now all gone? Hmph…

Dante's case should have ended in 6 months, tops. If race was not the leading factor, Dante would have been granted the Diversion Program and everyone would have gone home and would have been able to sleep that night. We have to make the laws work for us, Thurgood Marshall stated in the movie. That law should have worked for us, but race superseded the law. Race entered his case from the very beginning and continued throughout the duration of the case.

From the moment Dante entered the graveyard, had he been a white kid with blue eyes and blonde hair, there would have been suspicions and raised eyebrows. Questions would have been asked about his bizarre behavior, most likely before the automatic label of criminal entered the picture. More questions would have been asked before throwing him in the police car with more bruises on his body than anyone else at the scene. The elderly woman did state that she detected something was wrong with him, but she was still fearful, which was understandable. There was also the stereotypical assumption that I did not have private health insurance when the time came to hospitalize Dante, which I did. I could go on and on of how race played a role throughout, but I think that I have written enough, and one should get the picture.

Things will only get better through law and policy changes and the enforcement of them, I say.

Chapter 46
The Insanity Plea: Afterthoughts

After going through our situation and agreeing to plead the Insanity Plea for Dante, I do feel that I am now qualified to give an educated opinion on the matter. I agree with many scholars that the plea itself needs to be more defined and specific. I do not feel that a person who has committed a serious premeditated, heinous crime should be given the Insanity Plea, even if he has a mental illness. If there was time to carefully plan a crime, I do not think that the psychosis was acute. Dante does not feel as strongly as I do regarding this opinion as he has met quite a few in his travels at the Forensic Institute. He feels once these people are stabilized, they can be okay.

I feel that there should be harsher penalties for those persons who have committed those serious crimes, and they should either go to a regular prison with a focus on mental illness, or the role of mental health facilities in general should be considered more in depth than they currently are. As I write, I feel that prison reform has a closer tie to the role of mental health facilities. Many in prison have been diagnosed with a mental illness. Who goes to jail and who goes to a mental health facility should be considered more carefully.

Also, whether you are sent to prison via the Department of Corrections or to a mental health facility via the Department of Public Health, should not depend on the color of your skin or how much money that you have. This appears to be occurring in more cases than many may know.

I thought about a conversation that I had with an acquaintance who happens to be a black female judge and who is about my age. She informed me that the Insanity Defense in our state, and all over the country, is a delicate defense, so much so that she barely wanted to discuss it for fear of someone taking notice of her discussing the defense with me. In hindsight, it was a weird conversation, but she seemed to be saying that because it had been publicized in the media that our family was seeking the Insanity Defense, I needed to be careful regarding who I spoke with about it. The defense has been known to be twisted and construed and has had many different meanings for different court systems throughout the country, she said.

Having a lay person's knowledge of the defense at the time, I felt that it was the most appropriate defense for Dante given the situation that our family found ourselves in. We had been denied our first option, The Diversion Program. Yes, for Dante it was appropriate as it was written in the statutes. If others used the defense inappropriately, shame on them. The more I write, the more I understand the bigger problem.

Chapter 47
Planning For Dante To Come Home

The family continued to pull together as well as strategize next moves to assist in Dante's discharge. Big Dante had become more involved and was stabilized enough to become more of a support for me. He began to be the "stress buster man" that would take me out to enjoy movies such as the Block Blockbuster hit, *The Black Panther*. My daughter, who had been a sole source of support, was now engaged to be married and planning her wedding. She moved the date back once to assure Dante would be a part of the ceremony. She initially wanted him to walk her down the aisle. He had been her escort a few times when she was a teenager and I pushed her to participate in beauty pageants. Dante's sister later changed her mind and decided to let her dad walk her down the aisle. Dante would be an escort for one of her close friends.

Dante was unable to attend his sister's wedding which was a heartbreaker for all of us. The Senator offered to step in and try and see what she could do. I thanked the senator for her continued concern and informed her that since Dante's hearing for his temporary leave was scheduled to occur soon, we would save this battle for another day.

Dante did get the approval for temporary leave, but we had to have two hearings before this was accomplished. As of this writing, Dante is transitioning to a supervised apartment living arrangement. As Dante had never lived on his own, I was okay with this arrangement. As his mother, I had carried Dante until the age of 18. Living in an apartment with supports may work, I said to myself.

Chapter 48
Broken Hospitals & Mental Health Systems

As Dante was transitioning to an apartment, Big Dante relapsed. It was a difficult decision for me to decide to write this chapter. Big Dante had been doing so well. He did have brief hospitalizations throughout Dante's case, but had gone for a while without going to the hospital. He continued to struggle with completely accepting the diagnosis that had been given to him so many years earlier. I thought that he had finally reached a stage of acceptance until his last "relapse." As Dante had now received so much therapy, he was able to write his own essays and help me to write this book. He would counsel Big Dante and try to convince him to embrace the illness so that they could both help others.

Big Dante's last episode reminded me of how much work is still needed regarding mental health systems everywhere.

During his last relapse, the local hospitals that all knew Big Dante and his diagnosis decided that even though Big Dante had become psychotic again, they didn't feel that he was manic enough to keep and stabilize. The hospitals discharged Big Dante prematurely. He eventually got into an accident two weeks later. The hospital called and apologized for prematurely discharging Big Dante. I had been so drained from fighting and advocating on behalf of Dante that I did not want to take on another challenge with any of these local hospitals that obviously needed a refresher course on how to deal with the mentally ill. The mobile crisis unit was not much better. They were initially called to assist Big Dante with his relapsed psychosis and the answering service came on. "We don't work on weekends," they said. I am going to end this chapter with that. I'm drained.

As of this writing, Big Dante is in the hospital becoming once again stabilized.

Chapter 49
Dante's Day Ones

Before concluding this story, I would be remiss if I did not add a chapter that speaks to a few of Dante's friends who have hung in there with him over the past few years. I call them Dante's Day Ones because that is a hip-hop term that I didn't know of until I heard his latest hip-hop song that he had written while in the Community Re-entry Program. His Day Ones would visit and attend his court hearings and come to eat dinner with him on family nights when they could make it. They were all positive young black men, attending college or working. One enrolled in the military but still visited with Dante when he could.

Yes, Dante had his cousins and our family, but to have a few friends who initially had a hard time understanding how Dante had gotten into such mess but continued to support him was consoling to me.

I interviewed a couple of them specifically for this book. Being a young black male in society is difficult enough as there is a stigma around this factor alone. I wondered if Dante's friends had any general thoughts on what had occurred. The system is just corrupt, seemed to be the universal answer. It seems to be easy to get into the system and hard to get out, it was said.

I think that I wanted to interview these young men to also let them know to keep their heads up and to keep moving forward. I know that they did not need to hear that from me, because as I said, these young men appear to be headed in the right direction despite societal obstacles. Maybe I just wanted to tell them that to make myself feel better or maybe to make sure that they were okay. Either way, it was cathartic to do so for myself and maybe for them as well.

Epilogue
The Fight Continues

Even with increased awareness and continued research over the last 30 years, Mental Health Justice and Mental Health Reform have a long way to go.

I felt so alone in the fight to get people to understand our family's specific journey. As I mentioned previously, I did have many empathetic listening ears. However, the added element of race did not make the explanation any easier. Those in my own culture had difficulty connecting being diagnosed with a mental health disorder and being Black.

The stigma around mental illness remains large, even though there are many advocacy groups like NAMI, that have been created to try to reduce the stigma. The understanding of mental health disorders/ mental illness is lacking so much in society that I feel that it needs to be a part of junior high and high school curricula. It needs to join the fight that is occurring in our country to add Black History Studies.

People fear what they don't understand. That statement rings very loudly regarding issues of mental illness/mental health conditions. As I stated earlier, dealing with someone who has a mental illness and is untreated can be annoying. I will not change my mind on that.

I have realized while conducting my own research that the annoying behavior is a big part of the problem. That is why it is important for all of us to have increased awareness, including those who have been already diagnosed with a condition. In fact, those who have already been diagnosed and have the capacity to become a peer mentor to help others deal with their diagnosis should definitely do so. Truth be told, we all have the potential to be diagnosed with some form of mental health disorder at some point during our life time.

Increased awareness is needed at the least, to protect ourselves from ourselves. We are all in this together whether we want to be or not.

About the Authors

LaShawne Houston Sowell, LMSW, is the proud mother of two adult children. She has worked in the field of Social and Human Services throughout her adult life in various capacities, including with the State of Connecticut and as a Workforce Development Worker via her local Civic Association. She currently works with the Bloomfield Public School System and NAMI. Her most passionate work has been as an advocate for her community and for those who feel disenfranchised. Her most recent advocacy has been to raise awareness to eradicate the stigma of mental illness, more affectionately known as Mental Health Conditions.

She received her formal education from the University of Connecticut both undergraduate and graduate. She is most intrigued, however, by the training that she has received in recent years through the National Alliance on Mental Illness (NAMI). This training has allowed her to present in various forums regarding the latest research on helping to eradicate mental illness stigma.

Insanity Plea is her first published book and it is co-authored by her son Frederick D. Sowell Jr. It is her hope that eventually they can travel together to discuss and raise awareness regarding race, the triggers of mental health conditions, and combat the woes associated with these diseases.

Frederick D. Sowell Jr. is an aspiring Hip Hop artist who has created his own Mental Health Genre. He has written original songs such as "Positive Thoughts," "Revitalize," "Insanity Plea 2k16," and "Don't Worry Bout Me" to name a few. These songs are available on his Sound Cloud page @ SoundCloud.com/livinsowell. He is a graduate of the Metropolitan Learning Center (2013) and attended Manchester Community College where he declared a major in marketing since he felt that it would be needed for his Hip Hop career. He was voted "Most Likely To Receive a Grammy" by his high school senior class. He was also diagnosed with a mental health disorder just prior to graduating which prompted the need to tell our story.

Insanity Plea

Made in the USA
Middletown, DE
01 July 2020